THE HUNT FOR THE
ELUSIVE MASTERMIND

A MYSTERY SEARCHERS BOOK

BARRY FORBES

THE HUNT FOR THE ELUSIVE MASTERMIND

A MYSTERY SEARCHERS BOOK

VOLUME 8

By
BARRY FORBES

BAKKEN
BOOKS

ISBN 978-1-955657-25-9
For Worldwide Distribution
Printed in the U.S.A.

Published by Bakken Books
2022

PRAISE FOR BARRY FORBES AND
THE MYSTERY SEARCHERS
FAMILY BOOK SERIES

AMAZING BOOK! My daughter is in 6th grade and she is homeschooled, she really enjoyed reading this book. Highly recommend to middle schoolers. *Rubi Pizarro on Amazon*

I have three boys 11-15 and finding a book they all like is sometimes a challenge This series is great! My 15-year-old said, "I actually like it better than Hardy Boys because it tells me currents laws about technology that I didn't know." My reluctant 13-year-old picked it up without any prodding and that's not an easy feat. *Shantelshomeschool on Instagram*

I stumbled across the author and his series on Instagram and had to order the first book! Fun characters, good storyline too, easy reading. Best for ages 11 and up. *AZmommy2011 on Amazon*

Virtues of kindness, leadership, compassion, responsibility, loyalty, courage, diligence, perseverance, loyalty and service are characterized throughout the book. *Lynn G. on Amazon*

Barry, he LOVED it! My son is almost 14 and enjoys reading but most books are historical fiction or non-fiction. He carried your book everywhere, reading in any spare moments. He can't wait for book 2 – I'm ordering today and book 3 for his birthday. *Ourlifeathome on Instagram*

Perfect series for our 7th grader! I'm thrilled to have come across this perfect series for my 13-year old son this summer. We purchased the entire set! They are easy, but captivating reads and he is enjoying them very much. *Amylcarney on Amazon*

Great "clean" page turner! My son was hooked after the first three chapters and kept asking me to read more... Fast forward three hours and we were done! When you read a book in one sitting, you know it is a good one. *Homework and Horseplay on Amazon*

"Great book for kids and no worry for parents! I bought and read this book with my grandson in mind. What a great book! The plot was well done using the sleuths' knowledge of modern technology to solve this mystery." *Regina Krause on Amazon*

"Take a break, wander away from the real world into the adventurous life of spunky kids out to save the world in the hidden hills of the Southwest." *Ron Boat on Amazon*

"Books so engaging my teenager woke up early and stayed up late to finish the story. After the first book, he asked: Are there more in this series? We HAVE to get them! He even chipped in some cash to buy more books." *Sabrinakaadventures on Instagram*

DISCLAIMER

Prescott, the former capital of the Arizona Territory, is considered by many to be the state's crown jewel. Aside from this Central Arizona locale, the Mystery Searchers Book series is a work of fiction. Names, characters, businesses, places, events, and incidents are either the products of the author's imagination or used in a fictitious manner. Any resemblance to actual persons, living or dead, or actual events is purely coincidental.

Read more at www.MysterySearchers.com

For Linda,
whose steadfast love and encouragement
made this series possible

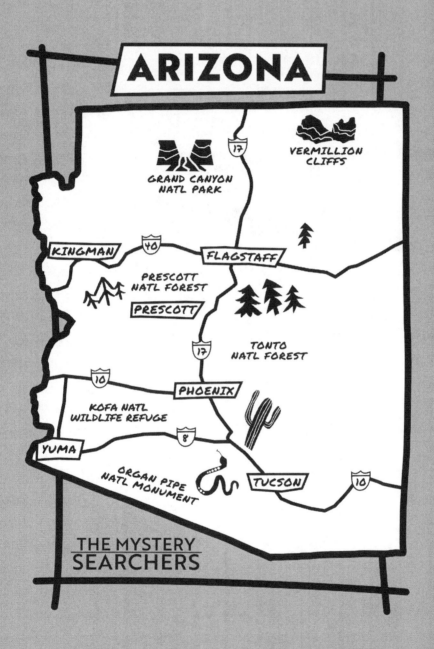

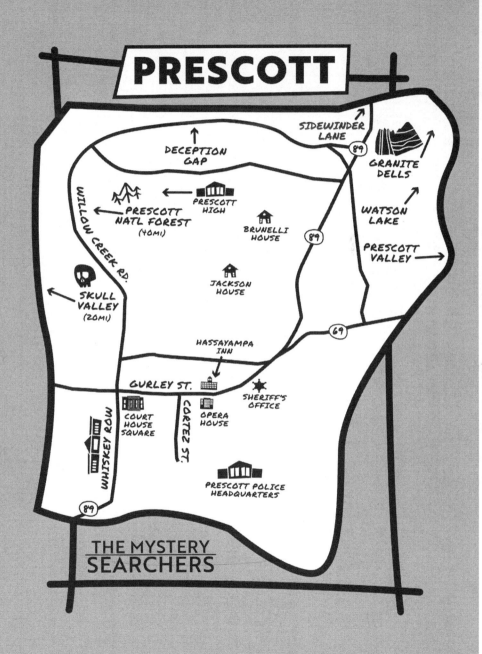

THE SET-UP

S ummer vacation had arrived—*At last!* thought Suzanne —in Prescott. It was a warm Monday morning in June, with piercing Arizona-blue skies stretching as far as anyone could see. *Promising!* A gentle cooling breeze wafted into town from the northern heights, fresh, forest-clean air that made everyone want to take a deep breath. Sounds of summer floated through the city's neighborhoods: birds sang, lawnmowers droned, and children shrieked with laughter. Somewhere in the distance a dog barked.

For Suzanne and her brother Tom, the Jackson twins, it was idyllic. The first day of their summer break from Prescott High was always the most evocative, delicious day of the year, bringing with it fond memories of summer vacations past and lots of plans for the days ahead.

After breakfast, the twins headed out toward Whiskey Row, Prescott's historic downtown district, a cluster of hundred-year-plus buildings lining one side of a long city block that had evolved into a tourist destination. Back in the roaring 1800s, the street had been famous—and infamous—

for its saloons, many of them now converted into art galleries and quaint shops. The twins planned to drop by Hall's Hardware, a corner store on Cortez Street, at the "request" of their father, Chief Edward Jackson—simply "the Chief" to all who knew him—of the Prescott City Police. He had surprised them at breakfast that morning—"Entrapped us!" as Tom laughingly quipped to Suzanne on their way out of the house.

"Any plans for today?" the Chief had asked quite innocently as he chugged down the last swallow of his coffee.

"Nothing big," Suzanne replied. "I might go shopping with Kathy."

"Not working at the St. Vincent de Paul Donation Center?"

"Nope, not this week. Mrs. Otto doesn't have enough used books for me to price."

"What about you, Tom?"

Tom glanced over toward his father with a raised eyebrow. "Pete and I talked about tennis, that's about it. First day off from school—time to take it easy."

"Great!" the Chief replied, beaming. "Because the picket fence needs painting, front and back."

The twins shot each other a look of theatrical despair. "Gee, Dad," Suzanne protested, "we just painted it a few years ago. It's the first day of summer vacation. Can't it wait?"

"Time out," Tom hastened to add. "That fence is in great shape—just ask Mom. In fact, it looks fantastic!" If there was one thing Tom disliked, painting fences appeared at the top of his list.

"Uh-huh," said their father cheerily. "Tom Sawyer time for you! Pick up four gallons of exterior white enamel at Hall's Hardware this morning. Charge it to my account." He grinned. "Enough for two coats. Shouldn't take you more than two days. Get a gallon of primer too—when you scrape off that loose paint, you'll expose bare wood."

One thing about the Chief: few people argued with him. Ever. Except for the twins' mother, of course. Sherri argued —especially when she thought her children's safety was at stake. And she won too. *Sometimes.*

An hour later, as they drove downtown in their Chevy Impala—an older model, but much loved—the twins kicked around the morning's curveball.

"Speaking for myself, I never even saw it coming," Suzanne moaned.

Her brother laughed. "Dad had it all figured out. See, it's the element of surprise, essential in fighting crime . . . and getting your kids to do chores. Did you message the Brunellis?"

"Uh-huh. I explained that management had conscripted us into forced labor. Maybe they'll be willing to help."

Kathy and Pete Brunelli were the twins' best friends. The four had grown close in elementary school; later, when they graduated to Prescott High, they had teamed up to solve local mysteries. Their successes had planted them on the front page of the city's hometown newspaper, *The Daily Pilot* —and often too. Along the way, the paper's star reporter, Heidi Hoover, had emerged as one of their biggest fans—and a good friend as well. It was Heidi who had dubbed the four-some "the mystery searchers." The name had stuck.

Suzanne drove as the twins headed downtown toward Courthouse Square, the cultural heart of Prescott. The quiet Central Arizona city of fifty thousand is renowned for its four-seasons climate and its gorgeous high-desert scenery, with rolling hills and mountains rising in the distance, and its proximity to the sprawling Prescott National Forest. Their route took them past police headquarters. As they cruised up Marina Street, four unmarked police cars—one after another, no lights or sirens on—whipped out of the police parking lot, cranked hard right, and sped away.

Tom sat bolt upright. "Hey, we've never seen that before. What the heck—"

"Here come two more." Sure enough, two more unmarked police sedans pulled out, heading in the same direction as the first four. And just as fast too.

"Did you see who was driving the last vehicle?"

"Uh-huh, Detective Joe Ryan," Suzanne replied. The twins had known the low-key investigator since childhood. The Chief often referred to him as "the best man on the force," and he enjoyed a well-deserved reputation for solving crimes. The mystery searchers had worked with him successfully on a number of previous cases.

"*Wait!*" Tom exclaimed. "Pull over, Suzie." The police station was already two blocks behind them.

"What for?"

"Something huge is happening. Let's go say hello to Dad."

A big old Caddy backed out of a parking spot on busy Courthouse Square. Suzanne nosed the Chevy in and the twins jumped out of the car. Tom plugged a few quarters into the parking meter before hiking back three blocks, mostly uphill on the city's slanting sidewalks. They pushed open the front door of police headquarters, just in time to see their father rushing out of his office.

Instead of his always immaculate blue uniform, he had changed into jeans and a short-sleeved shirt. And he wasn't armed. *Very unusual,* Suzanne thought.

"Dad!" Tom shouted, his voice ricocheting off the marble walls. His father stopped in his tracks and swiveled toward them.

"Hey, what are you two doing here?"

"We were going to Hall's, and we spotted all the police cars rushing off," Tom explained.

"We're just nosy," Suzanne admitted, only a little sheepishly.

The Chief smiled. "Well, since you're here— C'mon, I think you'll find this interesting."

Years earlier, the twins had decided to follow in their father's footsteps, an aspiration that he encouraged at every opportunity. Right now though, they were just trying to keep up with his long strides as he led the way out of the station.

The three Jacksons jumped into an unmarked cruiser. Relentless two-way radio chatter clamored on low volume— something about a stakeout.

"Our destination is only three blocks away," the Chief said as he pulled onto Gurley Street. "We don't want to draw attention to ourselves."

Suzanne sat in the front seat, staring intently ahead. "What's happening, Dad?"

"Ever heard of Ben Walters, the president of Prescott's Westward Bank?"

"I think so," Tom said, leaning in from behind. "Isn't Westward the sponsor of the Art Festival?"

"Uh-huh. Someone kidnapped his wife, Katrina, this morning, right after he left for work."

Suzanne gasped. "Kidnapped Mrs. Walters? From her home?"

"Affirmative. And we don't have a clue where she is now. Walters received a phone call when he arrived at his office— on his cell. Whoever the kidnappers are, they demanded all the money in the bank's safe—or else." The Chief pulled into a parking spot on Courthouse Square, just two spaces from the twins' white Chevy. "And we're talking about a consider-

Suzanne craned her neck. Someone moved slightly in the shadows behind almost-drawn curtains. "Barely."

"That's good—he doesn't want you to see him. Behind those curtains is Sergeant Bob Williams. He's one of six officers hiding in various places, including two on the roof of the Opera House. We've surrounded the dumpster, and there are ghost cars waiting on every major artery leading away from downtown."

"No way the kidnappers can escape without being tailed then," Tom said.

"None. And we've got a chopper in the air, too high up to hear right now. It'll follow the suspects anywhere."

"A chopper!" the twins chorused.

"Uh-huh."

"That's unusual for your department, right?" Tom asked.

"Yes. But this isn't the first time—we use them in rare cases, and this is one of them. The helicopter belongs to the Sheriff's Office, and the pilot is theirs too. You know what Sheriff McClennan's like—always happy to help. We can direct the chopper to follow the kidnappers' car, or cars, at a *very* discreet distance after they grab the money. It's unlikely they could shake us."

"This is a big story," Suzanne said, thinking quickly. "Can we clue Heidi Hoover in?"

The Chief shook his head. "Not a chance—way too dangerous. If word got out, it could endanger Mrs. Walters. Her safety is our number-one priority. Call Heidi when this is over—and I mean *all* over."

"What about Kathy and Pete?" Tom asked.

"Not yet," his father replied.

"Gee, Dad," Suzanne quipped, "a hostage situation really ties you up, doesn't it?"

"Sure does," her father replied seriously. "All we can do is shadow the kidnappers at a safe distance and hope they'll lead us to Mrs. Walters. The bank's got ultraminiature tracking devices sewn into the hems of the bags of cash—standard operating procedure these days. We'll track them, too."

Tom liked that—he was the mystery searchers' technology guy. He had learned to code in grade school and had become a founding member of Prescott High's prestigious technology club in his freshman year—the same year the team won a national robotics competition.

Suzanne's mind plunged ahead. "But there's no guarantee they'll release her alive. And if they think you're on their tail . . ."

"That's a fact." The Chief glanced at his watch. "But they have to know they're taking a big risk too. Kidnapping is a federal crime. And harming a hostage—that's a *very* serious crime. FBI agents are on the way from Phoenix. Do you remember Darren Baker?"

The twins nodded.

"Sure. He was at our house for dinner last year," Tom recalled.

"That's him. He's the Special Agent in Charge of Phoenix. A bright guy," the Chief said. "It'll be his case moving forward. My department will just be along for the ride, helping out the feds," he added ruefully.

Soon, silence shrouded the little apartment as the minutes dragged by, tense with anticipation. *It's like watching an hourglass,* Suzanne thought.

All three Jacksons stood, shoulder to shoulder, peering down through the blinds into the alley below. They focused on the big dumpster, mottled green with two top-loading swing doors—shut tight. *Which desperately need painting,* Tom thought. *Unlike our fence.*

Suzanne reached for her cellphone and silently counted down the seconds to ten-thirty. Outside, nothing. Inside the apartment, no-one said a word. No chatter on the Chief's two-way radio either. Suzanne watched the minutes tick by: 10:31 . . . 10:32 . . . 10:33 . . .

"Somebody's coming!" Tom whispered tensely. A burst of radio traffic erupted as a late-model black SUV pulled into the alley and glided to a stop beside the dumpster.

A man, appearing quite brisk and business-like in a two-piece suit, stepped out of his vehicle: Ben Walters. In his late fifties, medium-tall, with a neat mustache, thinning hair, and cheeks that cratered inward, the banker wore a worried expression. Glancing up and down the alley, he walked to the back of the SUV and popped the rear door. Eight fat, white money bags—*Bulging,* Tom thought—sat stacked inside. Walters raised one of the dumpster's two heavy lids and slowly rotated it backward, guiding it quietly down into place.

It took only a couple of minutes for him to toss the bags, struggling a little with their weight, into the dumpster, one at a time. Then he yanked the heavy metal door upward and gently lowered it closed. Once again, Mr. Walters scanned the alley both ways. Then he closed the rear door of his vehicle before sliding back into the front seat and slowly driving away.

"Where will he go now?" Suzanne asked.

"Headquarters. He'll spend the day with a technical officer, monitoring his cellphone. Just in case the kidnappers call or message him once more. They'll also monitor the signals from the tracking devices in the money bags."

"What if someone else finds the money before the kidnappers do?" Suzanne asked.

"Only one building uses that dumpster," replied her

father, "and that's this one. And we're watching. Anyone else who pokes his head in there will wish he hadn't, and quickly too."

"What's the next step for Prescott City Police now?" Tom wondered out loud.

"We wait," the Chief said.

AN HOUR DRAGGED PAST. ONE OR THE OTHER OF THE Jacksons stood guard, taking turns peering down through the blinds. The apartment grew increasingly warm as the day wore on. Tom checked for air conditioning, but there didn't seem to be any, and they didn't dare open a window. Meanwhile, the orange tabby overcame her fears and reappeared, treading softly into the tiny living room and jumping up on the couch. Suzanne stepped over softly and made a new friend. A little silver heart attached to the purring cat's collar read CUTIE.

At eleven-thirty, there was a sharp knock on the apartment door, which freaked out the cat again—it leapt off the couch and darted straight down the hallway. The Chief walked over to the door and opened it. "Darren, how are you?"

The two men shook hands as Special Agent in Charge Darren Baker exchanged greetings with the Chief. "I'm great, Ed. Good to see you. No action yet?"

"Nope, come on in. Just Ben Walters dropping off the money in the dumpster, exactly as we instructed him to, an hour ago. You remember Tom and Suzanne?"

"Oh, sure, the mystery searchers," Agent Baker replied, smiling and shaking hands with the twins. He wore a sharp business suit with a white shirt and tie. Solid but trim in his early forties, he exuded the aura of an experienced agent. "I sure do. Where are your two partners?"

"At home," Tom replied with a wry smile. "We weren't expecting anything like this."

"The twins stopped in at headquarters just as this was breaking," the Chief explained. "I figured they'd find it interesting."

"Well," the agent said, "you both told me you wanted to go into law enforcement someday. Now you can see it firsthand. Quite the waiting game, isn't it?"

"Check out the view," the Chief prompted. "There's the dumpster."

"No sign of the kidnappers?"

"Nothing."

"Interesting." He loosened his tie. "Hot in here. You know Walters?"

"Sure, I've met him once or twice—a straight arrow. His wife, Katrina, too . . . at social events. She's lovely. He's been the manager of the local branch of Westward Bank, four blocks south on Montezuma Street, since it opened nine years ago. Before that, he was running the main branch in Phoenix."

"Sounds like a step down in his career. Any idea why he made the move?" Agent Baker asked, flipping open a small notebook.

"Not sure. I'm guessing he and his wife fell in love with Prescott. Lots of people do."

"Anything else I should know about his wife?"

"Not that I can think of."

"I can think of one thing," Suzanne put in. "Right now, she must be very frightened."

· · ·

By 1:00 P.M., EVERYONE WAS STARVING. "TOM AND I COULD pick up some sandwiches at the Star Café," Suzanne announced. No objections to that idea. The twins ordered online using their father's credit card before heading out, with the apartment keys in hand.

If anything, traffic around busy Courthouse Square had increased even more then when they first arrived. There wasn't a parking place anywhere, and the shops—packed with summer vacationers—bustled with activity. Across the street, picnickers had spread blankets over the emerald-green lawns around the county courthouse.

As the twins strode past their white Chevy, Tom groaned. "Oh, man! We got a parking ticket."

"No wonder," Suzanne replied. "We've been parked there for more than three hours and never put another dime in the meter." She burst out laughing.

Tom glanced at her. "What's so funny?" She pointed to their father's car. Under his front windshield wiper was a parking ticket identical to theirs.

They both roared. "Oh, the irony. Dad will get a kick out of that," Suzanne said.

The sandwiches hadn't appeared at the take-out window yet. Suzanne took advantage of the wait to call Kathy.

"Where are you guys?" her best friend asked. "We've been calling you."

"Sorry. We stopped in to see Dad. He was leaving on a stakeout and invited us to come along. He made us put our phones on mute."

Kathy placed the call on speaker as Pete spoke up in the background. "Hey, that's gotta be interesting. What's it all about?"

"We can't talk about it." Tom replied. "Yet. But it's big. *Huge.* We'll fill you in later."

The sandwiches appeared. "Gotta go," Suzanne announced. "We're delivering food to the troops."

The twins headed back, crossing the intersection of Gurley and Cortez, threading their way through the crowds. Among them was a gaggle of excited small children and a woman herding triplets, all heading toward the Whiskey Row shopping area. After reaching the east side of the street, Suzanne stopped to pet a friendly yellow lab. "What a *beautiful* dog," she told the owner.

They headed over to the old bank building. At the narrow service entrance, the twins stood aside for two painters—one short and stocky, the other tall and slimmer—exiting the basement.

"Excuse us, folks," the short man said, leading the way. The painters were each lugging two five-gallon paint cans up the stairs and out to a blue cargo van parked in the loading zone.

Paint! In all the excitement, the twins had forgotten about the fence. *We still have to paint that stupid fence,* Tom silently grumbled. The twins raced up the stairs and unlocked the security door.

The turkey sandwiches were delicious, and the two-way radio dead quiet. The two officers spent most of their time deep in conversation, reminiscing about previous cases. The twins listened in, fascinated. Once again, time dragged. Watching and waiting.

Just after four o'clock, the two-way radio burst into life. The unflappable Detective Joe Ryan's voice came across, loud and clear. "Chief, we got a call from the communications center. The staff at the Best Western on Gurley Street found Mrs. Walters in one of the rooms—tied up, gagged, and handcuffed to a bedpost. I'm told she's okay. A patrol officer is running Mr. Walters over there just now. We're heading over to the dumpster."

The two officers and the twins exchanged looks. "What the heck—?" the Chief started. He raced out of the apartment and made his way down to street level with Special Agent Baker and the twins close behind. The foursome circled the building and worked their way round to the back alley.

Detective Ryan, four city officers and another FBI agent had arrived seconds earlier. At a signal from the Chief, an officer threw open one of the dumpster's mighty lids, allowing it to crash down behind. Everyone gathered around and peered into the depths.

There were a few seconds of stunned silence before Suzanne exclaimed, "I can't believe it! *They're gone.*"

INTO A TOMB

T om inhaled sharply. "Are they ever."

"How is that even possible?" Darren Baker asked.

"Surprise, surprise," the Chief said, pursing his lips.

"There's nothing down there except scattered newspapers," Detective Ryan said. He pulled himself up to the rim, flipped his legs over to the inside and dropped into the dumpster. He bent over and shoved a thin layer of paper aside, digging for the hard metal bottom. "Oh, man, check it out: a hole in the floor. It leads to a—"

"Tunnel?" Tom asked, peering down intently over the edge of the dumpster's side wall.

"Uh-huh. A narrow one too," Detective Ryan said. "No way can I squeeze through." He stared up at the circle of astonished faces above him. "Tom and Suzanne, you two are the slimmest of us all. Jump in here."

"You bet," Suzanne replied.

Now this is getting interesting, Tom thought.

The tall, willowy twins pulled themselves up, cleared the rim, and dropped into the dumpster. They fell to their knees and grabbed their cellphones, clicking on the flashlights.

Detective Ryan had thrust his head into a jagged hole cut into the metal floor. "I think there's a . . ." he said in a muffled voice. He came up for air. "Yeah, a rope ladder, hanging down against the tunnel wall. Can you two squeeze through here? Be careful—these metal edges are sharp."

"We can do it," Suzanne replied.

"Stick together and leave those flashlights on. We don't know who—*or* *what's*—down there. How do we communicate?"

"Open WhatsApp on your phone," Tom prompted. The three of them had used the app successfully on a previous case: the Deception Gap mystery. Scary memories of being hunted in the moonlit railyard came flooding back, but Tom pushed them away. *Work to do.* "We'll connect with you."

"Got it." Seconds later, they were all live on and connected on the app.

"I'm going first," Suzanne announced. She peeked through the hole, crudely cut into the floor, and projected her phone flashlight beam onto a dangling rope ladder. As she dropped her legs into the tunnel, her feet found a wooden rung that shifted perilously. She scrunched lower, ducked through the dangerous metal circle—it snagged her long, auburn hair and yanked for a second—*Ouch!*—before she was able to grasp the topmost rung with both hands. Then she pulled herself tight against the ladder as it wobbled side-to-side. Steadying herself, she started down, counting twelve rungs before reaching a dirt floor. *Safe.*

"Okay, Tom!" she called out. "It sways, but no big deal."

At the bottom of the tunnel, someone had hacked a three-foot square hole into—or out of—an old bricks-and-mortar wall. She knelt and projected her flashlight beam through the opening. "Whoa, there's a big basement down here." Then she crawled through the hole and stood up.

Seconds later, Tom stepped off the ladder and followed his sister into—well, wherever they now were. Silence shrouded them as a harsh, dampish smell assaulted their nostrils. The beams of their lights circled a dingy, dark, and cavernous area bounded by dusty, cobweb-covered red-brick walls, a stained concrete floor, and high ceilings. At the center of the space squatted a gigantic relic of a furnace. An old wooden bench stood pushed up against what Tom guessed must be the south wall, cluttered with dozens of tools, piled one atop the other. Stairs hugged the opposite, presumably north wall, heading up.

It was like walking into a tomb.

"This has to be the basement of the old Prescott National Bank Building," Tom said, his voice hushed.

"What makes you say that?" Detective Ryan asked over the three-way WhatsApp connection. His booming query echoed in the vast, almost-empty space.

"When we hit the bottom of the tunnel, we turned west, I think," Tom replied.

"Through a small opening cut into an old brick wall," Suzanne added. "Just a couple of feet from the bottom of the tunnel itself. Tom's right."

Tom spotted a pile of something creamy white along the basement wall, mere feet away. "*Check it out.* Money bags."

"All right . . ." their father's voice piped up in the background.

They walked over. Tom fell to one knee and bent down to look more closely at the bags. "Not good—they're all empty."

"Don't touch them," said Suzanne. "Evidence."

"Empty?" Detective Ryan asked. He didn't sound surprised.

"Decidedly so," Suzanne replied.

"Okay . . ." Detective Ryan continued. "Can you see stairs down there?"

"Yes."

"Walk up them and try opening the door at the top from the inside."

The twins headed up the long, wide set of steel stairs. A solid-steel door guarded the top, a close replica of the security door at the side of the former bank building's second floor. Tom hammered the push bar with his hip and pushed it open.

Right before them were familiar-looking stairs leading up to the ground level, and a second set—the same stairs they had trod earlier—that led to the upstairs apartments.

"We were right," Suzanne confirmed. "It's the building's service entrance."

"The door's open," Tom said.

"We're on the way," the detective replied.

Suzanne spotted a wall switch and flipped it up. A single ceiling fixture lit up below them.

Two minutes later, the Chief, Agent Darren Baker, and Detective Ryan—together with a knot of police officers, another federal agent, and the twins—all stood together in the basement of the historic Prescott National Bank Building.

Darren Baker introduced Special Agent Jim Reilly to everyone. "He'll head up the local investigation."

The twins watched and listened, taking in every word.

"The crime scene techs are on the way," the Chief said. "But this looks far from promising. All we have is a rope ladder in a manmade tunnel and empty money bags. No shovels, power tools, no construction materials, no bricks . . .

not even any dirt! These guys pulled off a heist like nothing I've ever seen."

"And the ransom money is gone," Darren Baker agreed. "Whoever they are, they're pros. Talk about deceptive. They knew exactly what they were doing."

"They sure did," Agent Reilly said. "And they must've even anticipated the GPS tags sewn in the money bags. This is far from their first heist, I'd say."

"How did they break through that wall without alerting anyone? Not to mention the pavement," the Chief asked.

"Good question," Darren Baker replied. "And cutting through the floor of that dumpster couldn't have been any fun, either. Someone put a lot of time into this heist."

"Ever remember another one like this?" Suzanne asked.

"No, I don't," Baker replied. "I mean, imagine the amount of planning this would take. Every detail . . ."

Tom shook his head. "While we were hanging around upstairs, they were down here—cleaning out the money bags."

"So it seems," the Chief said.

Suzanne groaned. "Oh, my gosh, I just realized something."

"Like what?" Agent Reilly asked.

"We saw them!"

Darren Baker shifted his intense gaze over to her. *"You saw them?"*

"Yes. Tom, remember? We picked up the sandwiches and then . . . those two painters were coming up the steps of the service entrance."

"Dead on, Suzie. I never connected the dots. I barely even looked at them. They were hauling stuff out, right?"

Suzanne's voice dropped almost an octave. "We should have noticed something was off. Remember those heavy five-gallon paint cans they were carrying out? They should have been *empty* if they were leaving a job site. The *money*, Tom. They dressed like painters, but their only project down here was that tunnel. Those guys were hauling out the cash! *Right before our very eyes.*"

4

DEAD ENDS

The Chief turned to Detective Ryan. "Joe, find the building's superintendent. Whoever that person is, we need to talk to him—or her—now."

"I'll get right on it." Ryan reached for his cellphone.

Thirty minutes later, the building superintendent paused at the top of the stairs and stared down. Five police officers, two FBI agents, three crime lab technicians, and the Jackson twins all eyed Charlie Varrick as he slowly descended into the basement. As he drew closer, the twins saw that he was a short, swarthy man in his early sixties with sunken cheeks and bulked-up shoulders. He wore eyeglasses and had his salt-and-pepper hair cut very short, almost military-style. They noticed too the perspiration beading on his forehead and staining the underarms of his short-sleeved shirt. Tom thought he looked like an aging weightlifter.

Nervous, thought Suzanne.

The Chief strode toward him. "Mr. Varrick?"

"Y-yes, sir," the man stammered as he came to a halt.

Everyone present gathered around, causing him to step back a foot. He licked his lips.

"You're in charge of this building?"

"Well, uh, yes, sort of."

"I'm Chief Jackson with the Prescott City Police. This is Detective Ryan. And these are Special Agent in Charge Darren Baker and Special Agent Jim Reilly, with the FBI." The four officers shook hands with him. "Any idea what's going on down here?"

The twins hung back, attentive to every word, hardly believing their luck. This, they knew, was a peek into their future.

Charlie's eyes darted around the room, trying to take everything in. "I . . .what—what do you mean? I don't understand."

The Chief pointed to the hole in the brick wall. "Someone broke through there and tunneled their way up to the street level. Do you know anything about this?"

"I—I don't, sir. No sign of that last time I was down. No, sirree."

"When *were* you last in this basement?" Jim Reilly asked.

"Uh . . . a few days ago, I guess. Wednesday comes to mind."

"Day or night?"

"I only work evenings normally, after five p.m., though I'm on call for tenant emergencies, of course."

"Doing what?"

"You name it . . . plumbing, painting, fixing stuff, janitorial duties. For the apartments and the commercial tenants too. I came downstairs that evening for a big wrench. Those are my tools on the bench over there."

"How long have you worked here?" Detective Ryan asked.

"Four years, sir."

"And before that?"

"I was the handyman with a traveling circus . . . for twenty-two years."

The Chief asked, "You don't come down here often?"

"Not in summer, no sir. There's no central air conditioning in this building, so there's little reason to come downstairs in the summer. All the janitorial supplies are in a closet on the main floor." He licked his lips again, obviously a nervous habit.

"So it's not broken, there just isn't any central air . . . ?" Baker confirmed.

"That's correct, sir. They converted the old coal furnace into this gas one decades ago. It provides heat for the building. The hot-water heater, which is electric, is under the stairs," he said, pointing. He shrugged. "There's a little annual maintenance every spring, but in summer it's rare that there's much in the way of servicing that needs to be done. The tenants each have a thermostat in their apartment, so they control their own heat. And of course—heck, Arizona summer, they hardly ever turn on the heat for months. Just on the occasional cold night, you know?"

"Notice anything unusual down here in the last week or so?"

"I've been off for three days. Before that, no, not a thing."

The Chief pointed up the stairs. "Who has keys to that door?"

"Well, I do, of course . . . and I have a janitorial assistant. He also replaces me when I'm off."

"So you've been off for the past three days and he replaced you. What's his name?"

"A young guy named Tim Smith. When he's on duty, he starts the same time as I do, five p.m. But there's no reason Tim would come down here."

"We need to talk to Mr. Smith," Detective Ryan said. "Do you have his phone number?"

"I sure do." He rattled the number off without a second thought.

Another officer raced up the stairs, cellphone in hand.

Darren Baker's eyes bored into Charlie. "No-one else has keys?"

"Well, the owner, of course."

"The owner?" Detective Ryan asked. "Who is that?"

"Cerrius Development in Los Angeles. They bought the building out of bankruptcy three years ago. But they're an absentee landlord, basically. They never send anyone out here . . . I mean, never. They manage the business out of their L.A. offices."

"Who handles the leasing?" Darren Baker asked.

"A local brokerage company, but I rarely see them either. The building's going up for sale soon, so that might change." Charlie wiped perspiration from his forehead with one hand. "There is . . . uh . . . one thing I should mention."

"What's that?"

"Someone stole my keys—and my wallet—from the janitorial closet upstairs. I reported it to the police."

Ryan asked, "When?"

"Two weeks ago."

The twins groaned in unison. "Well, that explains how they got in," Tom said.

NOT MUCH LATER, A UNIFORMED POLICE OFFICER ESCORTED A tall, thin young man down the stairs. "Chief, this gentleman is Tim Smith."

The officers introduced themselves and shook hands with him. He appeared to be about twenty.

He looks a bit nervous too, Suzanne observed. *Around the eyes . . .*

Detective Ryan led the questioning. "When were you last down here, Tim?"

He answered in a heartbeat. "Yesterday evening."

Even Charlie Varrick was taken aback. "Serious, Tim?"

"Yup."

"What brought you down here?" Detective Ryan asked.

"I didn't really come *down* here. When I came to work, I noticed the basement light on. First time in six months. No big deal . . . I figured someone had just left it on, accidental-like. So I unlocked the door and flicked the wall switch off."

"That would be at five p.m.?" Baker asked.

"Uh-huh."

The Chief stared at him. "But you didn't actually walk down the stairs?"

"No, sir. I opened the door and called out 'Hey!' No answer, of course—if someone had yelled back, I'd have jumped a foot. So I turned off the light and locked up. I never figured for a second anyone was down here."

"Never say never," Suzanne murmured.

Baker pointed to the hole in the wall. "And you know nothing about this?"

"Not a thing."

Minutes later, the questioning ground to a halt. The officers had reached a dead end, and everyone realized it.

"Should I have the lock changed, sir?" Charlie asked helpfully, holding up a key on a steel ring crammed full with many others.

Ryan palmed his nose, rubbing it with one hand. "I don't think so. But if you can lend us a copy for the basement door, we'd appreciate it. Thank you."

"No problem," Charlie replied. "Got an extra right here." He handed it over.

Charlie and Tim departed. Then, as Tom and Suzanne listened in, the officers huddled for a quick discussion.

"Thoughts?" Darren Baker asked.

"They're both clean, I bet," Detective Ryan said. "I'll run background checks, but I don't think they have any connection with the kidnapping."

Agent Reilly agreed.

So did the Chief. "Me too. What about you, Darren?"

"Yeah," he grunted, thrusting both hands into his pockets. Frustration had seeped into his voice. "Not much to go on, is there?"

The Chief paused for a few seconds. "Not yet."

"I wonder what Mrs. Walters could tell us about the kidnappers?" Suzanne mused out loud.

Detective Ryan arched an eyebrow. "Let's go talk to her."

5

DEBRIEFING

R ight after nine o'clock that evening, the Brunellis rushed over to the twins' house, eager to hear about their unexpected adventure. Tom and Suzanne had finished a late dinner, but their father had yet to arrive home.

Pete and Kathy rushed through the front door and into the kitchen. With their shared coal-black hair and olive-hued skin, the brother and sister appeared enough alike to be mistaken for twins and often were. Both were shorter and a little heavier than their tall, willowy friends. Pete, a year older than his sister, was the impulsive one who often moved too fast and talked too quickly. Kathy came across as a noisy, natural-born comic, her quick sense of humor a gift from her mother.

Kathy's eyes blazed with excitement. "Okay, you two. Now tell us what the heck happened. You disappeared for the entire day!"

Pete headed straight for the refrigerator and stuck his head in. Seconds later, the Chief walked in from the garage, winked at the other three, and stepped over to the fridge. "Anything look good in there?"

"Hi, Chief." Pete straightened up, wearing a silly grin. "That apple pie is sure tempting."

"I think you should have a slice."

"My thought, exactly."

While the twins' father rustled up food for himself, everyone migrated to the living room. The Chief soon joined them, with a steaming cup of hot coffee in one hand and a roast beef sandwich in the other. He laid claim to a seat on the sofa while Sherri sat down beside him. Tom dragged in an extra chair from the kitchen. The front doorbell rang.

"Come on in!" Suzanne called out.

Heidi Hoover pushed the door open and hurried into the living room, her tight black curls bouncing all around her head. "Hi, everyone. Sorry I ran late." Not only was the winsome young lady *The Daily Pilot*'s top reporter, but she had also assisted the mystery searchers with other cases. In one of them—the case that Heidi had dubbed "the secrets of the mysterious mansion"—her quick thinking and decisive action had led to their rescue. In another, she had shared in the reward money with the mystery searchers.

Heidi found room on the living room floor, leaned against a wall, and pulled out her oversize notebook and a sharp yellow pencil. Known as a person who rarely minced words, she didn't hesitate. "Okay," she said, "you've got my curiosity running wild. What's going on?"

The Chief sat back on the sofa, rolling his head to stretch out his neck and exhaling as he shifted into a relaxed pose. "The good news is that Mrs. Walters is doing fine."

"Mrs. Walters . . ." Heidi said, her nose twitching. "Who is she?"

Over the next hour, Tom and Suzanne—with a little help

from the Chief—brought everyone up to speed regarding the day's dramatic events. Soon enough, they reached the part about debriefing Katrina Walters.

Tom picked up the thread. "By the time we arrived at the station, Mrs. Walters was holding court." The twins chuckled. It had been obvious that the lady enjoyed being the center of attention. "After her husband left for work, the doorbell rang. Mrs. Walters peeked out and spotted a mailman holding up a small package in front of the camera. She spoke to him over the intercom, asking that he leave it at the front door. 'Can't do that, ma'am!' he yelled back, holding the package up. 'Ya gotta sign for it.'"

"Guess what?" Suzanne interrupted. "She unlocked the door, and two guys rushed her."

Sherri grimaced. "Oh, my goodness. That's horrible. *The poor woman.*"

"Oddly enough," Suzanne said, "they treated her well right from the start. 'Relax,' the 'mailman' urged, 'you'll be fine. We're just after the money.' The other guy—a six-footer the mailman called Tony—backed a SUV into the Walterses' garage. They pushed her into the back seat and drove away. Ten minutes later, the two men walked her into the Best Western on Gurley Street."

"The kind where you park right at the door of your room," Tom said. "She said they backed in, close."

"Do the Walterses own a security camera?" Heidi asked.

"They do," Tom replied. "Two of them. Pretty sophisticated system, uploads to the Cloud. The footage is automatically deleted after a month. Detective Ryan streamed the video files over to headquarters."

"Not much to go on . . ." Suzanne continued. "A late-model white Jeep SUV with a stolen license plate. Which might indicate the Jeep is stolen too. And the kidnappers wore disguises."

"There are a lot of white Jeep SUVs on the road," the Chief noted. "We ran a database check on stolen cars, but it didn't show. Possibly it started off as a rental before they switched the plates."

"In which case it might not have been reported as stolen yet," Tom noted.

"Exactly."

"What about the motel?" Sherri asked. "Did *they* have a security camera?"

"Sure did," Tom replied. "But the Jeep blocked the view. The kidnappers pulled her out of the *other* side of the SUV, out of view of the camera. They had planned everything."

Suzanne continued. "They told her not to worry—to stay calm. It helped that they had hot coffee and glazed chocolate doughnuts waiting for her. Her favorite kind too—they lucked out on the refreshments. The mailman introduced himself as Russell before Tony left to join a third member of the gang, someone Russell referred to as 'the mastermind.'"

"But not by name?" Heidi asked.

"No."

"What time did Tony head out?" Kathy asked.

"Right after Russell called Mr. Walters," Tom explained. "It was close to nine-thirty. He put Mrs. Walters on the throwaway phone—the kidnappers wanted to prove they had snatched his wife."

"They called his office number?" Pete asked.

"Nope. His cell."

Heidi's fingers raced across the notepad. This story, she would know, was *big*—one of the biggest in Prescott's recent history. She paused to message her editor: *Hold the press. Front page kidnap/ransom story coming tonight. Huge.*

"Did she get a good look at them?" Sherri asked.

"Kind of," Tom replied, glancing over to his mother. "The kidnappers wore oversize sunglasses and hoodies. Never took them off, not even inside the motel room. They wore fake mustaches as well—high-quality fakes, Mrs. Walters said, not Hallowe'en-costume glue-ons, but she could tell at close range that they weren't real. And they both wore latex gloves the whole time too."

"No fingerprints then," Heidi said.

"That's right," the Chief said between bites. He blew on the hot coffee and took another sip. "One interesting fact, both kidnappers had New York accents—Brooklyn, Mrs. Walters said. And she should know—she's a native of Staten Island."

"Staten Island?" Pete asked. "Where's that again exactly...?"

"Uh...that would be in New York City," Kathy said, shooting her brother a certain look. Which he has seen before. Many times.

"So noted."

Suzanne carried on. "Russell stayed with Mrs. Walters and Tony headed out, apparently for a rendezvous with the mastermind. Somewhere along the way, Tony must've exchanged his mailman duds for a painter's uniform. Then Tony and this mastermind guy headed out to the old bank building. We're certain they're the same men disguised as painters that Tom and I spotted coming out of the basement at lunchtime—just before one-thirty. One of them—the short guy who talked to us—must have been the mastermind."

"What makes you say that?" Sherri asked.

"Mrs. Walters said Tony is a six-footer. The guy leading the way out of the basement, the one who said, 'Excuse us, folks' was much shorter than that. So logically, he *has* to be the mastermind." Suzanne sat back, replaying the scene in her mind.

"They must have showed *after* we entered the apartment," Tom said. "No way did we see a cargo van when we first arrived."

"Russell, the mailman—he kept Mrs. Walters company for a few hours," Suzanne added. "'As long as you promise not to holler,' he said, 'I won't gag you.' She agreed. The gang had prepared well ahead. They had lunch—sandwiches, snacks, cold drinks, and two apples—just sitting there in the room, ready in advance. At noon, Mrs. Walters felt comfortable enough to eat with Russell—he played the part of a real gentleman. She claimed she felt safe the whole time."

"Picture this," Tom said. "Mrs. Walters played gin rummy and poker with the guy for hours on end. He talked little, but she had to watch him closely—he cheated!"

That sent everyone into gales of laughter. "That is *too* funny," Sherri exclaimed.

"Strange, huh?" Suzanne said. "She called him out twice, which he thought was hilarious. They got along well. Things changed at around one-thirty, when Russell's cellphone buzzed. It was a signal from the mastermind, he explained —'the boss.' Then he apologized, told her he'd have to tie her up and gag her, but that he'd phone the motel desk as soon as he could later in the afternoon and tell them to rescue her. He arranged pillows on the floor, so she'd be comfortable. Then he handcuffed her to the foot of one of the back bedposts. That was necessary, he told her, to give him and his gang plenty of time to escape the city."

"With the cash, of course," Kathy assumed.

"Right. He even made sure that the rope wasn't too tight on her wrists and the gag allowed her to breathe comfortably."

"Three members in the gang, right?" Pete asked. "No more?"

"As far as we know," Tom replied. "The two who kidnapped Mrs. Walters took orders from this mysterious third person—the so-called mastermind. He was the only one she never laid eyes on. Turned out, though, that besides getting caught cheating at cards, Russell himself seemed to be quite the experienced criminal. He never took off his oversize sunglasses, nor did he ever remove his hoodie. The guy did remove his gloves to eat and play cards, but the deck went into his pocket when they were finished. Then he slipped the gloves back on. He even wiped down the desk they ate and played cards on, even though she said he never touched the surface with his fingertips."

"That could indicate a criminal record," Kathy said.

The Chief grunted his agreement.

Heidi wondered, "No more communication from the kidnappers with Ben Walters after that first call?"

"Actually, yes," Suzanne replied. "Mr. Walters moved into police headquarters after he dropped off the money. He spent the day with one of the department's technical officers. The police and the FBI wanted to monitor his cellphone in case the kidnappers reconnected. Late in the afternoon, as Mrs. Walters was being debriefed, Ben's cellphone buzzed. It was Russell, calling to thank Mrs. Walters for being such a good hostage and—get this—'a terrific cardplayer.'"

Laughter burst out all around the room once again.

"You can't make this stuff up," Heidi murmured, almost to herself.

"Could you trace the call?" Kathy asked.

"Nope. Another throwaway phone," the Chief replied. "Seems they had a bunch of them."

"*Any* idea who they are?" Pete asked. He sat on the floor

with his back against his sister's easy chair. The empty pie plate lay beside him.

"It's just a theory so far," the Chief replied, "but Darren Baker—he's the FBI Special Agent in Charge of this case—believes it's likely an experienced New York gang, one that specializes in bank heists. The Art Festival ended on Sunday, and they seem to have known that the bank would be flush with extra cash."

"Oh, I get it," Sherri said. "That makes sense. How much did they get away with?"

"Just over three million dollars," said the Chief. "The Art Festival deposits topped up their cash on hand by a couple hundred thousand."

Pete let out a long, low whistle. Heidi's eyes bulged, and she wrote furiously.

Suzanne glanced over at her father. "I'm not buying it, Dad."

"Buying what?"

"The bit about the whole gang being from New York."

"Why not?"

"That painter . . . the one who talked to us in the service entrance—the 'mastermind' . . ."

"Uh-huh. What about him?"

"*He* sure didn't have any New York accent."

6

THE HUNT BEGINS

An eerie atmosphere had descended upon the Jackson household. For a few seconds, it felt as if the air had been sucked out of the living room.

The Chief's head had snapped up, but his voice remained calm. "You know what that means?"

"Sure. It means Tom and I were the only ones to have *seen* the mastermind. And no way was he from New York."

"I barely noticed the guy," Tom admitted. "But I *heard* him loud and clear, and you're right, Suzie."

"Well, you just threw a huge wrench into the FBI's theory," the Chief said. He chuckled, almost to himself. "Could be a local hit rather than an East Coast gang then."

Suzanne blinked. "Sorry!"

"Don't be. This is what investigative work is all about."

"That doesn't explain the guys with the Bronx accents," Heidi pointed out.

"True," the Chief admitted. "Not yet, anyway. Suzie, would you recognize the mastermind again?"

"Sure."

"Okay. First thing in the morning, you can sit down with our staff artist, Sergeant Noelle Pasteur. She's in charge of the Forensic Artists Unit. An artist's rendition of the guy's face will help the FBI immensely."

"I think the fact that he didn't have a New York accent," Kathy said, "is a big deal."

"Huge," Tom said. "He sounded like one of us, born and raised out West."

"Who owns the building?" Heidi asked.

"A development company in Los Angeles," Suzanne replied. "They purchased it from bankruptcy three years ago. The building's superintendent claimed their representatives never come near the place. Oh—and he said the building is going up for sale soon. I wonder why?"

"Could a bank employee be involved?" Sherri asked.

The Chief shrugged. "Who knows? Joe Ryan and the FBI will interview all the employees."

"We already know that only one staffer missed work today," Tom said. "Travis Johnson . . . he's a loan officer but also serves as the bank's security director. Right now, Johnson's on a road trip in Mexico with his wife. The FBI reached out to him, but wherever he's traveling, apparently there's no phone service."

"Three million bucks are missing," Pete said darkly, "and so is the bank's security guy. That's a heck of a coincidence."

"A couple using the Johnsons' passports landed in Mexico City two days ago," Suzanne said. "They're scheduled to check into a motel in Cabo San Lucas tomorrow night."

Heidi had another question. "Did the crime scene unit sweep the basement?"

"They sure did," Tom replied. "Nothing . . . except for one clue. They found a long auburn hair in the tunnel."

Suzanne grimaced. "Mine!"

Minutes later, Heidi closed her notepad and got to her feet. "Okay, that should do it. The story will be on the front page tomorrow."

The Chief stood up and walked the star reporter out to her car. "Heidi, we need your help. This is Prescott's *only* kidnapping for ransom that I know of and we don't have a single lead. Can you keep the story on the front page . . . for a few days in a row?"

"I'll do my best, Chief."

"Thank you. We'll keep you up to date with developments, so you'll have something to write about. One other thing. The bit about the FBI thinking it's a gang from New York . . ."

"Uh-huh . . ."

"For the time being, let's keep that *in* the story."

"Got it."

EARLY THE NEXT MORNING, TOM SAT OUTSIDE ON THE FRONT porch steps nursing a cup of coffee. He watched as the summer sun rose into a blue sky dotted by puffy white clouds. Right on time, *The Daily Pilot*'s Tuesday edition skidded face down along the Jacksons' driveway. Tom waved to the delivery girl and raced over, grabbed the newspaper, and flipped it over to the front page.

There it was—the lead above-the-fold front-page story, right where the editors had plastered it, just as Heidi had promised. Tom hurried back into the house, shouting, "The paper's here!"

Suzanne bolted downstairs and joined her brother and their parents around the kitchen table. Sherri rolled her eyes as Tom spread the newspaper right over the breakfast cups, saucers, glasses of orange juice, and cereal bowls. All four read silently at the same time.

The headline was set in bold, extra-large type:

Kidnappers Strike, Huge Ransom Paid
By Heidi Hoover, Staff Reporter

PRESCOTT — Mrs. Katrina Walters, wife of Westward Bank's president Ben Walters, was kidnapped by a professional team of gangsters first thing on Monday morning. The bank agreed to the kidnappers' demands and deposited $3 million in cash in a downtown Prescott dumpster, right behind the former Prescott National Bank building. In a shocking twist, the money disappeared down a hidden tunnel beneath the dumpster. Police and the FBI believe the kidnappers escaped with the ransom money. FBI Special Agent in Charge Darren Baker thinks a New York City gang targeted Westward Bank, in part because of its recently deposited receipts from the weekend's Art Festival.

"Wow!" Tom said, "Heidi wrote exactly what you asked her to."

"Heidi never lets us down," said Suzanne, nodding.

The Chief nodded. "Uh-huh. Those were Baker's exact words to me. Of course, thanks to both of you, the FBI has changed direction."

"They're focusing on Prescott, right?" Suzanne asked.

"Uh-huh," the Chief advised. "State-wide too. This 'mastermind' and his cronies could be anywhere—and *from* anywhere too."

"Including New York, accent or not," Tom said. "Is it okay with you if we stay involved with this case?"

The Chief hesitated. "Better talk to Joe Ryan first. He's our liaison with the FBI, so he'd be your point man."

The twins glanced at each other. *Splendid news.*

"Just be careful," Sherri warned. "You're dealing with professional kidnappers. They could be dangerous."

"We will," Suzanne said.

"I've heard that before . . . more than once too."

"Well," the Chief said, "they showed no signs of violence toward Mrs. Walters, but your mom's right. Be on guard."

"For sure," Tom said, looking quite serious.

"What's next?" Suzanne asked.

"You mean after breakfast?" the Chief replied with a wry smile. He stood and gathered up the newspaper, setting it on the kitchen counter. He glanced at his watch. "That would be your appointment with Noelle."

AN HOUR LATER, THE MYSTERY SEARCHERS PAIRED OFF INTO teams. Suzanne and Kathy trooped downtown to police headquarters while the boys headed out in the Brunellis' cherished Mustang—a grateful gift from someone who had benefited from the mystery searchers' sleuthing on a previous case. In an earlier call to Detective Ryan, they had learned that the police and FBI had already canvassed the historic downtown area in a search for surveillance cameras.

"We talked to every retailer first thing this morning," Ryan informed them. "Turned up three cameras close to the crime scene, but nothing that captured a view of the building's service entrance."

"Okay if we check around too?" Tom asked.

"Sure. Go ahead," Detective Ryan said. "But don't get out

in front of the FBI. Agent Reilly has moved into temporary offices here in the station. I'll be coordinating with him. If you discover anything, call me right away."

"Got it."

Minutes later, Pete pulled into a parking spot on Courthouse Square and fed the meter. The boys strode over to the Cortez-and-Gurley intersection before making their way to the service entrance. They stood out front, surveying the sights.

Two-and three-story buildings lined both sides of Cortez Street, all dating back a century or more. Ground-level retail space extended north and south on Cortez, and west along Gurley. Around the corner, toward the east, was the restored 1927 Hassayampa Inn, and across from the hotel sat the landmark Opera House—the site of one of the four friends' most dangerous cases. A never-ending stream of noisy summer visitors flowed past the boys, most on their way to the stores surrounding Courthouse Square and Whiskey Row.

Tom looked upward, focusing on a multitude of apartments on both sides of the street. A few sported old-fashioned balconies framed with wrought-iron railings. On one balcony, someone had layered laundry over a wooden sawhorse to dry.

"You know what, Pete? Detective Ryan said they checked all the surveillance cameras at the retail level. But what do you see up there?"

"Apartments—lots of 'em."

"That's a fact. And he never mentioned a word about them. Let's knock on a few doors."

That presented a challenge. All the ground-floor entrances to upstairs apartments had locked security doors, and almost no-one answered their doorbells. Three did and said, "No." *Click, click,* and *click.*

One two-story building had an unlocked door. The boys slipped upstairs and rapped on six apartment doors before an elderly lady answered.

"Someone asked me that same question a week ago," she replied to their question. She had a thick German accent and squinted at the boys through a three-inch crack between the door and the doorframe. A strong smell of cabbage soup seeped into the hallway. "I don't even know what a surveillance camera is. Would you like some tea?"

The boys excused themselves. "Everyone else is at work," Pete grumbled. He brightened with an idea. "Let's leave notes. Every mailbox is on the ground floor."

"Perfect."

They negotiated their way back through street-side crowds and jumped into the Mustang. Then they drove over to Pete's house and quickly created a flyer. It read:

IMPORTANT. WE ARE SEEKING INFORMATION RELATING TO a recent theft in downtown Prescott, just north of the inter-section of Cortez and Gurley Streets. If you own a surveillance camera, we would like to view any footage from yesterday, Wednesday, 10:00 a.m. to 3:00 p.m. Please call anytime."

"WHOSE NAME SHOULD I PUT ON IT?" PETE ASKED, GLANCING up from the keyboard.

"Yours and mine," Tom suggested. "And both cellphone numbers too."

Half an hour later, they stuffed a flyer into every mailbox close to the downtown intersection. It didn't take long.

"Now we wait," Pete said, feeling hopeful. "Bet anything we won't hear a thing until tonight."

Tom checked the time. "Let's walk over and check on the girls."

7

THE MASTERMIND

E arlier that day, Suzanne and Kathy had walked into police headquarters and headed straight to Detective Joe Ryan's office.

"Hi, ladies. Great to see you. Follow me, there're a couple of people who want to meet you." Their footsteps echoed off the walls as he led them to a smaller office down the marble hallway.

"Jim, this is Suzanne Jackson and her friend Kathy Brunelli. You'll recall Suzanne from last night's adventure. This is Special Agent Jim Reilly with the FBI."

The agent, a shortish, solid man in his thirties, looked serious and professional, with his square jaw, clipped short brown hair, and his white shirt and tie. Better yet, he displayed a friendly demeanor as he stood up. "My pleasure. I understand you're meeting with the forensic artist."

As the two girls shook his hand, Suzanne replied, "Thank you. Yes, I am."

"She got a good look at one of the kidnappers," Kathy said.

"So I heard," he said. "Great. We need all the help we can get."

"That's the truth," Detective Ryan said. "We're running background checks on everyone involved so far: Mr. and Mrs. Walters, Charlie Varrick, Tim Smith . . ."

"This afternoon we'll interview Westward Bank's staff," the agent added.

"There are only twelve local employees," Detective Ryan explained, "including Mr. Walters. We also need to chat with the building's owner. Jim will fly out to Los Angeles tomorrow morning."

The FBI agent doesn't appear hopeful, Suzanne realized.

A minute later, the girls met Sergeant Noelle Pasteur. "Come on in and make yourselves comfortable." They found seats around her desk and began to chat.

"This is a first for me," Suzanne said.

"Of course," the policewoman replied with a relaxed smile. With her short, dark hair, button-down blouse, and blue uniform—tunic hanging on the back of her desk chair— she appeared stylish and professional at the same time. *Oh, I would look good in that uniform,* thought Suzanne.

"Please, call me Noelle. I think you'll enjoy this—the finished product is often pretty accurate. I'll ask you a series of questions and sketch as we talk. We'll preview photos of specific facial parts and see if I can match the image in your mind. I understand you had a close brush with one of the kidnappers."

"Yes, for sure."

Noelle pulled out a large sheet of matte-finish drawing paper and laid it across her artist's desk, an adjustable surface that sloped slightly down toward her waist. "How old is this man?"

"I'd say about sixty."

"Tall or short?"

"On the shorter side . . . I'd guess five foot eight."

"Did he have a full face?" Noelle was already sketching the outlines of a man's face.

"Sort of. Not chubby."

"Smooth or lined?"

"I—I'm not sure. Maybe just a few wrinkles? Around his eyes and on his forehead."

The image began taking shape on the paper.

"Was he clean-shaven?"

"No. A little stubble, I think."

"Hair color?"

"Graying, but not all gray yet."

"Lots of it?"

"Hard to say—he had a painter's cap on. I recall thin hair, long and stringy, hanging down over his ears and down his neck."

Noelle's fingers traced back and forth in sure, rapid strokes. She employed a set of sharp charcoal pencils, each one a slightly different degree of gray-black, to create a clear facial image rendered with subtle shading, accented by white highlights where she allowed the paper to show through. Soon, she pulled over a sizable book and turned to a couple of pages showing various chins. "Which one most looks like his?"

"Well . . . this one."

"Let's find his eyes."

The two searched stock images of each facial element and selected the closest match. Squinty eyes appeared, topped by bushy eyebrows. A broad nose emerged. Ears peeked out amid stringy hair. Dimples surfaced.

Half an hour slipped by before Noelle held up the large sheet. "Is this close?"

Suzanne stared at the man's face with amazement. "Yes, it sure is. His cheeks might still be a little thinner . . ."

Noelle erased a bit to pull in the facial contour before asking, "Now?"

"Wow," Suzanne replied. Somehow the face made her feel uncomfortable. "That's him."

"So there he is," Kathy said. *Not a friendly face at all. No surprise there.*

The officer signed and dated the front of the sheet, right below the portrait's neckline. She flipped the page over. "You sign and write the date here too, Suzanne, in case we use this as evidence at some point. We need to prove that this image preceded his arrest—if we arrest him."

Just then, the two boys walked into Noelle's office. The girls introduced their new friend, and the boys shook hands with her. Suzanne proudly showed them the finished product. "That's him, for sure," she said. "Isn't it amazing?"

"That's the guy who talked to us?" Tom asked.

"Dead on."

At that moment, Pete's cellphone buzzed. He stepped out of the office and into the hallway. "Hello?"

"Hey, my name is Lawrence Perrault," a voice said. "And I've got a surveillance camera pointing down onto Cortez Street."

The mystery searchers deserted both their cars at police headquarters and hiked over to Cortez and Gurley Streets, just three blocks northwest and, mostly, downhill. The caller had said he rented an apartment three stories up. Their hopes soared: he lived across from the service entrance.

Pete pushed an intercom button at street level. A loud

49

buzzing sound emerged from a metal panel as the door clicked open. "C'mon up," a disconnected voice rang out. "I'm in three-eleven." The boys followed Suzanne and Kathy up two flights of stairs, then three apartments to the left.

The door was open. "In here!" Mr. Perrault called out. The foursome stepped into a small living room that smelled of stale food. A nerdy-looking man in his early twenties, seated in front of a keyboard and multiple computer monitors, swiveled to greet them. He was a clean-cut guy with piercing blue eyes and short hair spiked up, dressed in jeans and a white T-shirt, no shoes or socks. "Sorry, it's a little tight in here. Find a seat—I hooked the camera up to my large-screen monitor. I'm Lawrence, and you are . . . ?"

The mystery searchers introduced themselves. Pete found a spot on the floor and the others squeezed onto a sofa as Tom explained their role in the case. "You heard about the kidnapping, right?"

"Did I ever," Lawrence replied with a smile. "Right across from my apartment, no less—that caught my attention when I read the story. I work evenings at the Sheraton Hotel . . . so I was sitting here when it all happened. Didn't have a clue!" He sighed, glancing over to the twins. "Your father is the chief of police? That means you're the mystery searchers, right?"

"Yes," Suzanne replied.

"You've heard of us?" Pete asked, trying hard not to puff up just a bit.

"Sure. I've read the newspaper *and* the online stories. You guys have made the front page a few times. And you use tech to help solve mysteries. I like that—I'm the evening tech geek for the hotel. What are you looking for now?"

A fellow techie. Tom liked him instantly. "A cargo van pulled into the loading zone across the street. Sometime yesterday between ten a.m. and three p.m. If possible, we need to see that vehicle—"

"And whoever was driving it," Kathy added.

"Okay." Lawrence swiveled toward his gigantic wall-mounted screen as his fingers raced across the keyboard. "I'm getting a little action out of that camera—it's on the balcony, pointing close to straight down. The quality of the hi-def image is so good, it's almost scary. A week ago, some guy asked me to search for footage. From a car accident, no less . . . but this is my first kidnapping. I set it up when I moved in, thinking I might catch something cool, someday. And I was right!" He glanced back at everyone and laughed out loud, a pleasant, ringing sound that bounced around the room. "I'll start at ten a.m. and scan through."

On the monitor, a never-ending parade of people and vehicles swirled past at high speed. The camera's cone of view caught a wide swath of the street, starting at the inter-section and extending north a couple hundred yards. Cars and trucks stopped and started. A traffic jam froze every-thing for a few seconds. A motorcycle pulled to a stop; the driver made a quick, jerky phone call before zipping off. Two buses came and went.

At twelve-forty, a dark-blue cargo van zipped into the loading zone. The driver's-side front door opened, and the driver started out. Lawrence froze the video. "Is that your guy?"

Without even realizing it, everyone leaned closer toward the monitor and its high-def still. The camera had caught a weird, downward view of the driver, frozen just as his left foot hit the pavement. Suzanne stared hard at the man, frozen half in and half out of the vehicle, as she examined his painter's overalls and cap, and the stringy hair hanging down over his neck and ears. "Yes . . . Yes!"

The van was caught dead center in the video frame, showing just a hint of a graphic on its driver's-side panel in a top-down view, a series of letters—seven, including an obvious apostrophe, but the sharp angle made the word impossible to read.

"No way to read that logo, or whatever it is?" Pete asked.

"Not a chance," Lawrence said. He touched PLAY.

The driver finished exiting the vehicle and circled around to the back of the van. He stopped and turned, looking back.

"It's definitely him!" Suzanne said. "But something's . . . different."

"Maybe your memory of the sketch is actually throwing you off," Kathy offered. "His face looks awfully similar to the drawing."

"You could be right."

A second man, tall and thin, emerged from the passenger side of the van. "Tony," Tom guessed. The man wore an identical painter's uniform and a floppy cowboy hat tilted steeply down to hide his face. Within seconds, both men had disappeared into the darkness of the building's service entrance.

"Notice they carried nothing in with them," Tom said.

Lawrence hit FAST FORWARD. Cars, trucks, a motorcycle, two buses, and pedestrians all whipped by at ramped-up speed. Then, at 1:22 p.m., Suzanne shouted, "There *we* are!" Lawrence hit PLAY to slow the footage down to normal speed.

The camera had captured the twins on their return trip to the apartment, takeout bags in hand. They came to a polite stop before the service entrance, allowing the kidnappers room to exit the narrow passageway. The driver glanced over to Suzanne and mouthed something. *"Excuse us, folks,"* replayed in her mind. For the first time she realized his face had registered surprise when he saw her.

Tom had the same thought at the same time. That twin thing. "He didn't expect to bump into anyone."

As the twins disappeared into the entranceway, the second "painter"—Tony, the taller man—walked to the van, his face still hiding behind the brim of the hat. The two men yanked open the van's rear doors and deposited the four big paint cans in the van's cargo area: five-gallon size and made of gray metal—contractor-grade. Although the paint cans looked heavy, the thieves handled them with ease. After slamming the double back doors shut, Tony fiddled with a lock for a few seconds as the shorter man jumped into the driver's seat.

Seconds later, the driver back-checked for traffic. Then, for some inexplicable reason, he leaned far forward over the steering wheel, glanced across the street, and looked straight up through the windshield . . . one, two, three stories. They could see his face clearly as he peered straight up, directly into Lawrence's camera lens. The corners of his mouth twitched up and his eyes locked onto . . . *something.* Somehow, the sinister look—and the weird smile—threatened and taunted at the same time. Then it dropped away, his mouth drooping back to normal. He glanced back to the driver's side rearview mirror before pulling into the near lane of traffic.

"Okay, what was *that* all about?" Suzanne wondered aloud. Her skin crawled.

"Awfully creepy, isn't he?" Kathy said. It wasn't really a question.

"Beyond creepy. . . But something's—*off*," Suzanne said. "He's—he looks *different* from how I remember him. I can't put my finger on it. The way I described him to Noelle, and the way she drew him—that isn't exactly how he looks to me in the video."

"What do you mean?" Tom asked.

"I dunno. Guess it's because his face was frozen on the screen and you get to stare at the guy. When I saw him in the service entrance, he didn't seem so—so cold and eerie, almost plastic, like one of those dolls in a scary movie. Plus he looks like he's been eating too many corn dogs lately. And did you get a load of those long sideburns? I hadn't noticed them."

"Could just be the camera," Lawrence said.

"Could be," Suzanne agreed glumly.

"Well, they came empty-handed," Tom said, "and left with four paint cans . . ."

"Paint nothing," Kathy quipped. "Those boys just made a withdrawal—a big one!"

8

A CONTEST

The mystery searchers had just said their goodbyes —"Thanks, Lawrence!"—when Suzanne received an incoming message. She glanced at her screen. "We're wanted at police headquarters. Pronto."

They quickly hiked back. An officer at the front desk pointed them toward a meeting room, where they found Detective Ryan, Special Agent Jim Reilly, and Heidi gathered around the conference table.

"We ran Noelle's sketch over to Mrs. Walter's house," the detective said. "She never laid eyes on that guy. Based on what Russell told her, that means the suspect you spotted in the service entrance must indeed be the elusive 'mastermind.'"

"So," Reilly said, "we've asked Heidi to run the pic of this so-called mastermind in tomorrow's newspaper."

"Good timing," Tom said. "We just located footage of the guy from a downtown surveillance camera."

"Together with the kidnapper called Tony," Suzanne

added. "We think the camera caught them taking the ransom money out of the building's basement."

The two officers glanced at each other. "Well, that was a miss on our side," Ryan mused. "Where did you find it?"

"On the balcony of a third-floor apartment," Kathy replied, "across the street from the service entrance."

Ryan nodded. "We talked about those apartments but figured the angle would discourage anyone from installing a camera. Good for you."

"Here you go." Tom handed over a thumb drive. The detective plugged it into his laptop and hit PLAY. Everyone huddled around the screen as the scene played out. Then they ran it a second time.

Special Agent Reilly shook his head in disgust. "How easy is that? They're walking out with three million dollars, and no one looked at them twice."

"Including me," Tom said.

"It's amazing how the driver matches Sergeant Pasteur's sketch," Detective Ryan noted. "Any idea why he's looking upward like that before they drive off?"

"We asked ourselves the same thing," Tom replied.

"That broad-brimmed cowboy hat hid Tony's face," Detective Ryan noted. "We're no farther ahead in identifying him. And because of his disguise, Mrs. Walters couldn't help either." He glanced over to the FBI agent. "No way to read that logo on the side of the van?"

"Not that I'm aware of. We need a better visual. Ideas, anyone?"

Pete drummed his fingers on the conference table, unsure of himself. "I've got one . . ."

"Like what?" his sister challenged.

"Well, consider this," Pete said, leaning forward. He rested both elbows on the table and clasped his hands together.

"There are hundreds—thousands—of people downtown during the summer. The busiest time is later in the morning, early afternoon. What are folks doing?"

"Sight-seeing, shopping..." Suzanne replied.

"Uh-huh. A lot of them are summer visitors," Kathy said.

Pete flashed a toothy grin. "Yup. And they're taking pictures... and videos, with their cellphones. Lots of them."

"*Pete!*" Tom exclaimed, "you're on to something. That van might show up in the background of someone's footage."

"Now you're talking."

"I like it," Jim Reilly said. "But how do we reach those people? How can we access that footage?"

"I can do a story..." Heidi started.

"Or a contest," Pete said.

"A *contest?*" Suzanne asked.

"Sure. Something like this: Best scenes shot on Wednesday, ten to three p.m., at the intersection of Cortez and Gurley Streets. The winner gets a hundred bucks." Pete sat back and grinned, feeling rather proud of himself.

"It's a *great* idea," Kathy said. She gave her brother a rare high-five.

"I agree," Detective Ryan said. "Prescott City Police will supply the cash prize. Can you run with it, Heidi?"

"You bet I can. I'll tie it into the newspaper's 'Celebrate Summer in Prescott' feature series. It'll appear on the front page tomorrow morning."

"It could work," Agent Reilly said, deep in thought. He turned to Ryan. "Of course, we could tip off the kidnappers that we're on their tail—here, in Prescott. Not in New York City."

"Sure. But any press from *The Daily Pilot* is going to spook them. Our only real leads are the sketch, the Jeep, and that cargo van. I think we should go for it."

The agent nodded. "Okay. It's possible the kidnapper-thieves wouldn't even spot the contest article—or connect it to the mastermind. Can you separate the two stories, Heidi? Get them far apart, but still on the front page?"

"Consider it done."

"All right. Let's go for it."

On Wednesday morning, the foursome met at the Brunellis' house for coffee and sweet rolls. Noelle's sketch of the elusive mastermind stared out at them from the newspaper. "Have you seen this man?" read the top headline. His image, exposed to thousands of *The Daily Pilot's* readers, had to pay off. It just *had* to.

"Someone has to know this guy," Pete said. "It's only a matter of time. He's toast."

The Brunellis' mother, Maria, was in the kitchen putting on more coffee. "You already ate half a loaf," she teased. Pete's appetite was legendary.

"Mom, you weren't listening!" Kathy's laughter rang out.

The contest announcement ran toward the bottom right corner of the front page, with all the details below a small caption:

Celebrate Summer in Prescott Award

The Daily Pilot is running a $100 prize promotion in search of the best summer scenes in downtown Prescott. If you captured stills or video last Monday—between 10:00 a.m. and 3:00 p.m. around Cortez and Gurley Streets—forward your footage to our star reporter, Heidi Hoover, right away. We'll announce a winner on Friday!

· · ·

"SHE INCLUDED HER EMAIL ADDRESS AND SEPARATED THE TWO stories," Suzanne mentioned. "The kidnappers might not connect the dots."

"That's what the investigators are hoping," Tom said.

By 10:00 a.m., Heidi had three contest entries, none of them offering anything even close to the shot of the van that the mystery searchers were hoping for. Seven more entries dribbled in over the course of the day: images of children, selfies, and food. Courthouse Square showed up twice, its emerald-green lawns dotted with picnickers. But there was no cargo van with any identifying graphics. In fact, even the famous old Prescott National Bank building didn't make the cut.

Worse, not a single call came into the newspaper regarding the elusive mastermind. *Not one.*

"Which, when you think of it," Suzanne groused, "is amazing. I mean, the guy is distinctive looking, don't you think? Anyone would recognize that face. What the heck?"

"Maybe he *is* a New Yorker," Kathy said.

"Doubtful."

At six o'clock, Heidi texted the mystery searchers and Detective Ryan before heading home. *No luck today.*

EARLY THE NEXT MORNING—*VERY* EARLY—LONG AFTER Suzanne had gone to bed, an intermittent buzzing woke her from a sound sleep. She sat up and grabbed her cellphone from the bedside table. *Heidi.*

Instantly wide awake, she propped her pillow up and clicked on the incoming message. Date and time-stamped Thursday, 12:50 a.m., it read, *Bingo! We've got a winner named Hannah. Check it out.* Suzanne's adrenalin raced as she touched the screen. A noisy video clip popped up before she quickly muted the audio: a daytime scene downtown, the Cortez-Gurley intersection with the former bank building in the background.

Hannah had begun recording on the intersection's north-west corner as she trod east, cranking her camera in a circular panning motion, generating a clip that bounced as it swept the scene—and capturing a dark-blue cargo van slightly to her left. The van blurred past before people walked in front of the lens, clearing just in time as Hannah locked onto her target: Suzanne—*Me!*—falling to one knee and petting the dog. Tom stood above and to her right, his back to the camera.

But in the clip's initial moments, an unmistakable bold white logo on the van's driver's side panel had whipped past: PABLO'S PAINTING. *Yes!* Suzanne crowed inwardly.

Suzanne jumped out of bed and raced across the hall, shaking her brother awake.

"This'd better be good," Tom muttered grumpily as he sat up.

Suzanne tapped PLAY and handed him the phone without saying a word.

Seconds passed as her brother focused. "Oh, wow. Pablo's Painting. Now we're onto something."

"You got that right."

"That's us."

"Uh-huh."

Tom replayed the clip and froze a scene. "You can see the license plate on the back of that van."

"Yup. But the vehicle's moving so fast, the plate is a total blur—no way to read it."

Tom's feet hit the floor. "I bet I can fix that."

9

CLUES

P rescott High's technology club was the proud owner of an extensive software library. One recent addition boasted a toolkit used to enhance video footage, perfect for school plays and sporting events.

"Great stuff," Tom explained to his sister. "It got a serious workout this spring. Best of all, I can access it online."

At 1:18 a.m., he downloaded the software to his laptop. No problem reading the van's logo again, of course, but the license plate presented quite a challenge. The van was only visible in five seconds of very bouncy footage captured by a moving camera.

Tom used the software's video stabilization feature to isolate and freeze a single promising frame, then zoomed in to magnify the rear of the van by two hundred percent—as if the camera had been twice as close to the vehicle as it really had been.

"Whoa," Suzanne exclaimed over her brother's shoulder. "You can *almost* read it. It's an Arizona plate, for sure."

Tom's fingers tap-tapped across the keyboard, the only

sound in the dead quiet of the house. Over the next fifteen minutes, Tom deployed various visual effects, adjusting the brightness, contrast, vibrance, and saturation of the screen capture. Not all the effects produced useful results, but over time the image grew clearer . . . not enough to read the plate, but *better*. Last of all, Tom tried the sharpening effect.

Finally, the Arizona plate emerged in bold, beautiful color, still fuzzy but readable: B435672.

Without thinking, Suzanne whooped out loud—*At last!* That brought their father out of bed, calling from the top of the stairs. *"What* are you two doing down there?"

Minutes later, the Chief ran the license plate number through headquarters. "It's a U-Haul rental van, registered in Phoenix. I'm going back to bed." He headed upstairs.

"Dad's a little grumpy this morning," Tom whispered to his sister with a grin.

"That's weird," Suzanne said, ignoring the dig. "It's a good-size cargo van, but it's sure no U-Haul. They're always painted white—with U-Haul logos plastered all over them."

LATER THAT SAME THURSDAY MORNING, THE FOURSOME gathered to search online for Pablo's Painting. *Nothing.* They checked Arizona's Corporation Commission for a listing —zero.

Worse, an early morning call to Detective Ryan confirmed Suzanne's doubts. U-Haul had reported the license plate missing from one of their rental vans—but no missing vehicle.

"Stolen?" Kathy asked.

"Stolen," Detective Ryan repeated matter-of-factly. He put the call on speakerphone. "Jim Reilly is with me."

"Where from, and when?" Tom asked.

"Phoenix," Reilly answered. "U-Haul reported it missing one day before the kidnapping, but they say it could have been stolen up to a week earlier. Even if we had run the plate on Monday, it wouldn't have shown up. Whoever pulled off this job knows how law enforcement works."

The foursome felt deflated. *"Crud,"* Pete said. "We're back to a dead end."

"We couldn't find any listing of Pablo's Painting either," Suzanne said. "It must be made up."

"We figure they stole the van," Pete said, "and then printed and stuck the logo on the side of the van themselves."

"And then slapped on the stolen plate," Kathy said.

"I'm sure you're right," Detective Ryan said. "That's our guess too."

"By the way," Agent Reilly said, "the background checks arrived on Mr. and Mrs. Walters, Charlie Varrick, and Tim Smith. All clean, no criminal backgrounds, no financial irregularities, either . . . not even a parking ticket. Today, we're running checks on every other employee at the bank."

"Including Travis Johnson?" Suzanne asked.

"Affirmative."

"What's next?" Tom asked.

"Finding that cargo van," Detective Ryan said. "It's possible the kidnappers left evidence behind. Maybe even fingerprints. And we expect the Jeep won't be far away—maybe we'll even find the two vehicles together. Prescott City Police has patrol officers searching the city."

"We've alerted the Yavapai County Sheriff's Office too," Reilly said. "Something will show up . . . it's just a matter of time. After all, they're not on the way to New York—right?"

. . .

LATER, THE FOURSOME SAT OUTSIDE THE SHAKE SHOP, THEIR favorite meeting spot since junior high, which featured outside picnic tables and delicious hamburgers and shakes.

"Just coffee for me," Suzanne ordered. "Too early in the summer for a shake."

"Plus all that sugar's bad for you anyway," Kathy said, fighting the temptation.

"Make mine chocolate," Pete ordered, never giving it a second thought.

Tom sipped on a steaming cup of coffee. "Pablo's Painting sounds like the owner could be Hispanic, right? Let's knock on a few doors and ask if anybody's heard of them. Plus, we have the sketch of the mastermind—we'll show that around too."

Prescott has a good-size Hispanic community, and the mystery searchers all spoke better-than-average high school Spanish. They canvassed several of the city's neighborhoods that same afternoon. Whenever someone answered their front door, they held up the forensic drawing of the master-mind and asked, "*¿Conocen ustedes a este hombre? ¿Han oído hablar alguna vez de Pablo's Painting?* Do you know this man? Have you ever heard of Pablo's Painting?"

The answers never varied. "*No. Y no. Nunca.* Never."

"Time for dinner," Pete said, three hours later. "This guy doesn't exist—and neither does Pablo's Painting."

THE THEORY

F riday morning dawned to the melancholy sight of low-hanging clouds that had gathered overnight, the heavily overcast sky threatening a deluge. The Jackson family breakfasted together before the Chief abruptly left on an emergency call.

An hour later, Pete and Kathy banged on the front door before heading straight into the kitchen. They beat a torrent of rain by seconds; thunder and lightning boomed in the distance. As the mystery searchers gathered at the kitchen table over coffee, a gloomy feeling permeated the room. They had arrived, Suzanne pointed out, at what looked like a dead end.

"Why didn't *anyone* recognize him?" she asked for the second time. "Thousands of people read *The Daily Pilot,* but not a soul called in. I mean, that's just . . . *weird.*"

"Well—" Pete hesitated. "There are only two main options."

"True," Suzanne said, adding a dollop of cream to the bitter brew concocted by her brother. "We've covered all that. First, the mastermind is a local guy with a low profile, and now hiding out somewhere around town."

"Very unlikely," Kathy said with a thumbs down. "*Someone* would have recognized him and called the newspaper."

"That leaves option number two," Suzanne said. "The guy's an out-of-towner, and now probably long gone—with the loot."

"That's possible," Pete said, nodding. "New York . . . Phoenix . . . who knows? The FBI's first theory could have been on target."

"We'll never solve this mystery," Kathy said with a sigh. The gloom deepened. Leaden seconds marked by the kitchen clock ticked by.

Tom sat back, deep in thought. He ran fingers through his thick, auburn-colored hair before leaning forward, arms on the table. He pushed his coffee cup aside. "I wasn't going to mention this—not just yet, but—I've been considering a third possibility."

Suzanne pulled a face. "Listen, hotshot, are you keeping secrets? Whatever do you mean by that?"

Kathy looked at him in surprise. "Like what?"

He glanced over to his best friend. "Pete, remember yesterday, when we finished canvassing the neighborhoods?"

"Uh-huh."

"You said something remarkable."

"I did?"

Kathy poked her brother in the ribs with an elbow and grinned. "That's a first."

"You said, 'This guy doesn't exist.' That's what woke me up in the middle of the night. So I lay there thinking—"

Pete was impatient as ever. "About *what?*"

"Like, what the heck are we missing?" Tom took a deep breath and opened both hands, palms up. "Think about it.

The kidnappers exit the service entrance and bump into Suzie and me. Two days later, one of them—the mastermind —gets his mug on the front page of the newspaper. Not a single person calls in to identify him."

"Which points to an out-of-towner," Suzanne said.

"Sure, that's possible. Except for the fact that the guy tossed a serious enigma into the mix."

"We're all ears," Kathy said, pushing her chair closer.

"Remember Lawrence's video, the moment when the mastermind got behind the wheel and stared straight up toward the camera?"

The three others glanced at one another. "Sure," Suzanne said, recalling the man's weird, creepy face.

"Uh-huh. I wondered about that. Pretty strange, wouldn't you say?"

Kathy hesitated. "Maybe."

"No maybe about it," Tom said pointedly. "He had to have done that on purpose."

"Whatever for?" Suzanne demanded.

"He had seen Lawrence's camera before, and he *wanted* it to capture his image. In fact, he made sure it happened— which explains that crazy little smile. The guy *counted* on the police working their way to Lawrence's door. He *wants* them to know what his face looks like."

"Or the FBI," Kathy said. "Though it was *us* actually. But I don't get it. Why would he do that? It makes no sense."

"Sure it does." Tom swiveled back toward Pete. "Remember when we first canvassed for surveillance cameras? Before we set out the flyers?"

"Sure."

"And the elderly lady who asked us in for tea? The one who said someone else had knocked on her door asking about a surveillance camera, just a week earlier?"

"Yeah," said Pete. "So what?"

"Lawrence told you the same thing, right?" Kathy recalled with a start. "That some guy had rung his intercom asking about a surveillance camera with regard to a car accident."

"Exactly." Tom leaned back and took a deep breath. "They're all pieces of a jigsaw puzzle—a brilliant one too. Suzie, you sensed something was off, something *fake*, about the mastermind's face when you got a good long look at it in the still frame at Lawrence's. Something you didn't detect when we ran in to him briefly in person. The frozen face in the video is what tipped you off."

"You got that right," Suzanne said. "I thought the guy almost looked—"

"Plastic," Tom said, grinning. "That's what woke me up. And then I realized that Pete nailed it. *That person doesn't exist.* It's a façade—a disguise—maybe one of many—that he slaps on for criminal activity in public. That explains those ridiculously long sideburns. He counted on the police seeing him on the footage—but he didn't count on running into us in person!"

"Whoa," Suzanne said, "I think you're onto something. I remember he seemed really surprised to see me. I—I couldn't quite figure it out . . . but you're right!"

By now, Tom had their attention—big-time. "The FBI said the kidnappers were professionals. No way would a pro show his actual face on purpose to a surveillance camera. Never. Put it all together, and you've got one heck of a devious plan."

"Okay," Pete said, "I'm all in. But why would he bother? I mean, why not just lie low and spend the cash?"

"I think that's pretty obvious," Tom finished. "Don't you?"

Seconds ticked by before Suzanne broke the silence. "Yeah, I get it. It's that New York thing, isn't it? The mastermind wants the FBI to chase a nonexistent person who has fled back to New York City."

"Precisely. What did the kidnappers tell Mr. Walters? That they'd release Mrs. Walters unharmed, only after they had all escaped Prescott with the dough."

"Sheesh!" Kathy exclaimed. "At which point the FBI would put all their efforts into hunting in New York—"

"Pursuing a nonexistent gang," Pete said, finishing her thought. "Meanwhile, the mastermind is relaxing nearby, enjoying life. Holy doodle!—as Heidi would say."

Tom nodded. "He might not be alone either."

"There's one hole in your theory," Suzanne said. "The two guys who nabbed Mrs. Walters had Bronx accents."

"That's true," Tom said. "And I considered that. But if the mastermind is a local guy, he'd need professionals to pull off the job, right? I mean, how many criminal types can execute a flawless kidnapping and make it appear easy? It's quite possible the guy reached out to the underworld in New York City. Having Bronx accents—unmistakably real ones, according to Mrs. Walters—was all part of the plan."

Pete shook his head. "Right down to their native tongues."

"Uh-huh," Kathy agreed. "A false flag, and even the FBI fell for it. But guys like that don't come cheap."

"Not an issue," Suzanne reckoned out loud. "Whoever the mastermind is, he waved a whole lotta dollars at them. Some big chunk out of three million, in fact!"

The gloominess in the kitchen dissipated as the mystery searchers' laughter and excited voices rang out. Soon enough, the four were on their feet high-fiving one another.

"You know what's an amazing coincidence?" Suzanne asked, glancing toward her brother.

"What?"

"If the mastermind hadn't spoken to us in the service entrance, we would never have caught on."

"That's a fact," Kathy said.

Tom agreed. "Funny how that happens. All it takes is one simple mistake."

Pete pulled out his cellphone. "Time to call Lawrence."

A MYSTERY MAN

Heavy clouds still threatened overhead, but the driving rain had traveled southward. The foursome parked on Gurley Street and fought a damp, gusting wind, thankful they didn't get drenched.

When they arrived at his apartment, Lawrence had already slid his sofa closer to his gigantic monitor, pulled up two folding chairs, and dimmed the lights. Pete had briefed him minutes earlier by phone. "The guy is *into* it," he said to Kathy in the car on the way over.

The boys handled introductions before the monitor lit up, chasing away the day's gray dullness. On the screen, days flew by in seconds as Lawrence scanned backward at high speed through each day's footage.

Then he froze the image. "That's him."

The mystery searchers edged closer. A shadowy night-time scene illuminated by a single weak streetlight captured a medium-tall man arriving from the direction of the Hassayampa Inn, just as he turned the corner and headed north on Cortez Street. He wore dark clothes: a black jacket and pants, with a dark-colored baseball cap pulled low over his brow. Even if the footage had been shot in broad daylight, his facial visibility would have been minimal. But at nighttime? *Hopeless.* The poor illumination, a cap yanked low, and the severe camera angle all worked against them.

As the man reached the service entrance of the former bank building, he glanced back over both shoulders quickly before crossing the street to Lawrence's security door. The foursome held their collective breath. With the camera pointing almost straight down, an overhead light revealed nothing but the top of a Diamondbacks baseball cap with the team's logo on the brim. The mystery man punched an intercom button. Seconds passed.

"Notice that he's hitting the panel more than once," Lawrence said in a low voice. "I'd bet anything he's searching for the owner of the security camera—*me*."

"You're right," Suzanne said. "See: his head's moving as if he's talking to someone. . . Now he hits the panel again . . ." Two minutes later, the man yanked open the door and disappeared.

"Bingo," Lawrence said. A half-smile crossed his face. "He found me."

"What did he say?" Pete asked.

"On the intercom? He said something like, 'Sorry to bother you. I had a minor car accident recently and wondered if you might have happened to catch it on a surveillance camera.' I said, 'Sure, come on up. We can look.'"

"Whoa, how simple was that," Kathy said. The audacity of the man amazed her.

"Uh-huh. Next thing I know, this weird guy's sitting in my living room, right there on the sofa. He told me the aggrieved party had threatened to sue him, and he needed evidence."

"Weird?" Tom asked, sitting straight up. "In what way?"

"I dunno. He wore his cap with the brim pulled down way low. I could barely see his eyes. No idea how old he is. He was a little . . . *strange*."

The mystery searchers exchanged glances. It felt slightly creepy to know that a reputed criminal had sat right where they were sitting now.

"He sat on this sofa?" Kathy asked, sliding closer to her brother.

"Yup. Right where you are."

"Oh, joy," Suzanne said.

"Did you find footage of the accident?" Tom asked.

"Nope. I couldn't find anything that looked like the accident he was describing. He claimed his car had barely brushed the other guy's. So he went on his way and I forgot all about it. Until now." Lawrence blinked a few times as he turned toward them. "He set me up, didn't he?"

"He sure did," Kathy said. "Would you recognize him again?"

"Sort of. I mean, he never took off that baseball hat, the brim pulled down low . . . all on purpose, right?"

"Mm-hmm," Suzanne said. "Obviously. Could you pick him out of a lineup?"

"Doubtful."

Tom drummed his fingers on the chair. "So it appears we have another suspect, someone partnering with the short guy with the stringy hair—the mastermind—and they're both working to lead investigators astray in advance of the kidnapping. Could it be Russell? Tony's too tall to be this guy, right?"

"*This* guy is taller than the mastermind, if not by much," Kathy said. "But we still don't really know who either one of

73

them are. And he doesn't have to be one of the kidnappers. There could be four men involved."

"Maybe *this* new guy is the real mastermind," Pete suggested.

Kathy grimaced. "I feel a headache coming on."

Suzanne had a question for Lawrence. "You work evenings. How did this guy figure out you'd be home?"

"I dunno . . . maybe he got lucky. My off days are Sunday and Monday. He hit me up on a Sunday night."

Tom asked, "Can you fast-forward to when he left?"

"Sure."

It didn't take long. In the footage, the front doors of Lawrence's apartment building opened, and the man walked out. Instead of retracing his steps, though, he turned north and hurried to the next apartment building.

"Where's he going?" Kathy asked.

"The elderly lady we met lives two doors north," Pete replied.

"Oh, sure. Got it. Of course."

"Now let's track him when he comes out," Suzanne said.

Lawrence fast-forwarded once more. Seven minutes later in real time the man reappeared, heading south to Gurley Street before vanishing around the corner.

"Who told him about your camera, do you think?" Kathy asked.

"It's easy to spot from ground level," Lawrence replied. "You guys saw it, right? But I'm guessing he wanted to make sure it worked."

"So, when he heads up the street, the guy is hunting for a second camera, a backup," Suzanne said.

"Wait. *What?*" Pete said. "I'm missing something. Why?"

Lawrence shrugged. "My guess? Just in case. What

happens if my camera is out of commission? His subterfuge plan would fail—"

"And the FBI would put more resources on the case in Prescott," Tom finished.

"I'll tell you what," Lawrence said as he stood up and stretched. "I've never spotted a surveillance camera next door. He's one thoughtful dude, isn't he?"

"But not as smart as he thinks," Pete said. "We'll get him. It's only a matter of time."

Minutes later, the meeting ended with the mystery searchers thanking Lawrence warmly and promising to keep in touch. They walked away with the clips they needed on a thumb drive. A quick discussion followed on the sidewalk outside.

"We need to check with that elderly lady," Tom said.

Pete grinned. "The one who asked us in for tea?"

"Uh-huh. She talked to the guy, in person too, not just over her intercom. She might remember something helpful."

"I'm not a tea guy," Pete said. "But Kathy loves the stuff, don't you?"

"About as much as you do."

"We'll do it," Suzanne volunteered for both girls. They had proven themselves to be sensitive interviewers on several previous cases.

Tom pointed to the apartment building two doors north. "She's upstairs, apartment two-oh-one. I don't remember her name, but it's on the mailbox."

"When you escape, we'll be at the police station," Pete said with a flourish. "It's time we told the investigators how to run this case!" He laughed.

"You do that," Kathy said with a giggle, "and they'll run you right out of town."

THE DUCK WALK

An hour later, Detective Ryan and Special Agent Reilly agreed that the mystery searchers had stumbled onto something big.

"Your jigsaw puzzle isn't proof positive," the agent remarked. "But overall, I think it makes sense."

The boys grinned. "Thank you, sir," Tom said.

"But who *is* this new mystery guy, anyway?" Ryan asked with a dismissive gesture. "Now we've got *four* suspects, not three."

"No idea," Pete said. "But we know what he was after. He wanted to send all of us on a wild goose chase."

"It worked, too," Agent Reilly said. "My New York office is busy chasing down leads. I'll reroute them toward Tony and Russell, the two guys with Bronx accents. This fourth guy's interesting, but it's the mastermind we really want." He paused. "Whoever he is."

"He'll be in control of the money," Detective Ryan said, nodding. "How are we gonna flush him out?"

"Make him feel nervous," Tom suggested. "Let him know the heat's on, here—"

"I like that," Pete said. "Not in New York City, but *here*— in Prescott."

"If he thinks we're onto him," Tom replied, "it could force him into the open. Or even panic him into making a bad move." The twins had learned a lot of theory and procedure from their illustrious father—not to mention from similar successful gambits they had devised in order to solve previous cases.

The agent nodded. "What do you think, Joe?"

"I like it. Tom, call Heidi Hoover. Ask her if she's available to join us."

HALF AN HOUR LATER, SUZANNE AND KATHY RUSHED INTO THE meeting room and found seats around the conference table.

"Guess what?" Kathy teased. "Mrs. Guggenheimer is eighty-seven years old and sharp as a tack. She had a little surprise for us."

"Like what?" Tom asked.

Suzanne explained. "When our fourth mystery suspect knocked on her door, she didn't have a clue what he was talking about."

"That's what she already told us," Pete said. "She doesn't know a security camera from a toaster."

"Right. What she *didn't* tell you is that she could identify the subject if he ever showed again."

Detective Ryan lit up. "She'd recognize his face?"

"Nope," Kathy said. "His walk."

"His walk?"

"Uh-huh. When the guy knocked on her apartment door, which she keeps chained, she opened it and peered out—

through a three-inch gap. Same guy, of course—baseball cap pulled down low, dark jacket and pants, polite and well-mannered. She didn't find him creepy. After she sent him on his way, she watched him walk down the hall to the next apartment. She noticed that he walks like a duck. Splay-toed. Kind of a waddle."

"Why didn't we see that in the footage?" Pete wondered.

"The camera angle," Kathy explained. "The way she describes his walk, you probably have to see him from behind."

"Plus the footage is dark," Tom said. "You can't really see his legs most of the time, never mind his feet."

"She'd recognize that walk again?" the FBI agent asked.

"For certain."

"Did she come up with a description?" Agent Reilly asked.

"Not much," Kathy replied. "Medium-tall, middle-aged, dressed nicely, but the baseball hat hid his face the whole time."

"And no accent," Suzanne added.

Heidi knocked on the conference room door and stepped in. She greeted everyone before spreading her notebook out on the table. A few minutes slipped quickly by as the others briefed her.

When they finished, she said, "This is a weird case, isn't it?"

"That's a fact," Detective Ryan agreed.

"Heidi," the FBI agent said, "we'd like to change the focus of the story. Rather than claiming it was a New York gang that kidnapped Mrs. Walters, we'd like to announce that investigators have discovered it was a local job."

"And that the kidnappers have employed subterfuge and disguise to mislead the FBI and Prescott City Police," Joe Ryan added.

"Is this official?" Heidi asked.

The two men exchanged glances. "It is," Agent Reilly said.

"Okay. No problem. I'll have it on the front page tomorrow morning. But if you don't mind my asking, what are you expecting to happen?"

"We're hoping your story will make them panic a little," Tom replied. "And that then they'll do something careless to tip us off."

"Like what?" Heidi asked.

"Like we haven't got a clue!" Pete admitted. *"Yet."*

LATER THAT EVENING, RIGHT AFTER DINNER, THE CHIEF'S cellphone buzzed. He had a habit of walking away as he took calls but soon returned to the kitchen.

"Okay, thanks . . . uh-huh. We'll head out there now." He disconnected and eyed the twins. "That was communications at headquarters. Park rangers found both vehicles."

"Cool," Tom replied. "Where?"

"Watson Lake, parked side by side."

"Just what Detective Ryan figured," Suzanne reminded everyone.

"The crime scene techs are on the way out there now," the Chief said. He walked into the living room and slipped his shoes back on. "Let's go."

"I'll call Pete," Tom said, reaching for his cellphone.

Suzanne touched Heidi's name on her phone's screen.

THE BRUNELLIS LIVED EVEN CLOSER THAN THE JACKSONS DID to Watson Lake, a popular hiking destination a few miles north on Highway 89, so they arrived ahead of their friends. Within minutes, Pete and Kathy pulled into a gravel parking lot at one of the trailheads. Just yards away was the lake's shoreline, punctuated, they knew, by huge, rounded granite boulders, many of them half submerged, alternating with narrow promontories flanked by tiny islands. In some places, shrouded pyramids of rock rose majestically, almost cliff-like, from the water's edge.

Five crime scene technicians had arrived earlier in two well-equipped police trucks. Already, powerful LED lights on telescoping stands lit up the area like daylight as technicians scoured the scene. Meanwhile, other team members worked on the locked doors of each vehicle, prying them open and forcing their way into the front seats.

"That didn't take long," Kathy said.

Three more vehicles pulled up in quick succession. The Chief parked his cruiser clear of the action, farther up an incline. The Jacksons piled out just as Detective Ryan and FBI Special Agent Reilly drove in, parking parallel to the Chief's car. Heidi followed right behind them.

"We should have figured this out before," Joe Ryan remarked.

"Maybe not," said Kathy. "I think . . . maybe the kidnappers are sending us a message."

"Yes," said Pete, catching on. "Another distraction . . ."

"Such as . . . ?"

"Such as, 'We abandoned these vehicles here and swapped them out for others on our way out of town.'"

"Yeah, I get it," the Chief muttered. "Meanwhile, they're probably watching the football game at a watering hole downtown."

"I wonder if they left anything interesting behind for us?" Jim Reilly asked.

Heidi shadowed the crime lab team. Meanwhile, the

mystery searchers used their cellphone flashlights to illuminate a circular path around the investigative area.

"Nothing here but gravel and a bit of litter," Pete grumbled. "Wish we could see inside that van." Technicians wearing gloves and white overalls worked their way through the cargo area.

Guided by her cellphone flashlight, Kathy trailed along closer to the shoreline. "Hey, check this out."

"What is it?" Suzanne asked.

"Clothes, I think . . . *yes!* Painters' uniforms. Look."

"Don't touch them," Tom counseled as he rushed up.

"Why not?" Pete said. "There can't be any fingerprints, can there?"

"Sure there can," Suzanne counseled. "Fingerprints in paint. We have to let the crime lab deal with this."

13

HOT MONEY

W hen they gathered on Saturday morning to review the case, the mystery searchers agreed that the identification card Kathy found in one of the painter's uniform pockets was just a plant. In this, they concurred with the police department and the FBI. They had instantly recognized the tiny ID photo on the phony Arizona driver's license: the "mastermind."

"Another false flag," Tom said, "to throw the investigators off."

"Our buddy, the man without an accent," Suzanne said.

Pete wondered where the phony license had come from.

"According to the Chief, they're pretty common," Tom said. "People sell them at swap meets in Phoenix. Plus, you can purchase a driver's license on the Dark Web. It's counterfeit, but it sure looks real, doesn't it?"

The man already identified as the mastermind had flashed his sinister little smile when his ID shot had been taken.

"Notice he has shorter sideburns in this photo," Suzanne said.

A shiver ran up and down Kathy's spine—the guy creeped her out. "He's deliberately taunting us."

"You got that right," Pete said, nodding. "No evidence in the cargo van or the Jeep?"

"Not much," Tom replied. "They found lots of dirt on the cargo van's floor. That might explain what happened to the debris they dug out from the tunnel. They're still running fingerprint checks, but my guess is they'll strike out."

The morning's newspaper consumed most of their discussion. Heidi had come through with another stellar article:

POLICE HAVE A STRONG LEAD ON ONE KIDNAPPER. THE MALE— believed to be the gang's mastermind—disguised himself to draw FBI and police officials away from a local investigation. Authorities now believe at least two Arizona suspects arranged the kidnapping and robbery, assisted by experienced East Coast criminals with Bronx accents. The picture shown is of one suspected perpetrator wearing a disguise. Prescott City Police are asking anyone with information to call the department's tip line.

"IF THAT DOESN'T STIR THEM UP, NOTHING WILL," KATHY SAID. The expression on Suzanne's face caught her attention. "What's wrong?"

"Wrong? Nothing. I just realized something."

"Like what?" Tom asked.

"The picture of our buddy jogged a memory. It was the

clip from Lawrence's video . . . the one where they're loading the paint cans into the van."

"Yeah, so what?" Pete motioned her impatiently.

"Tom, remember when Mr. Walters tossed those eight sacks of money into the dumpster?"

Her brother nodded. "Uh-huh."

"They were heavy, weren't they?"

"You're not kidding," Tom said. "He struggled with each one of them."

"He sure did. But in the video, the two kidnappers hauled out four giant paint cans we figured had to be full of cash, two each . . . right?"

"Right!" Kathy said, her voice rising with excitement. "Logically, there should be two sacks' worth of bills in each can. So each one would be about twice as heavy as one of those money bags by itself, but they handled them as if they were full of feathers. They set them in the back of the cargo van with no effort at all."

Pete's eyebrows arched up. "It doesn't make sense, does it?"

"*Dang,*" Tom exclaimed, locking eyes with his sister. "Suzie, you're onto something. We all missed that. Do you know what that means?"

Suzanne grinned. "Well, it could mean the money never really left the bank—"

"And is still hidden in that basement!" Kathy cried excitedly.

"*Let's go!*" Pete shouted.

JUST AFTER ELEVEN THAT MORNING, DETECTIVE RYAN unlocked the basement security door of the historic old building and swung it open. "C'mon in." He led, negotiating his way down the wide stairs to the basement floor. It was the Brunellis' first time there.

"Where's Special Agent Reilly?" Pete asked.

"He's in Los Angeles, interviewing the building's owner. Flew out early this morning."

The sour dampish smell the twins recognized all too well assaulted their nostrils as the group probed every nook and cranny of the cavernous space.

Tom pointed out the kidnappers' entry point to Pete and Kathy. The hole in the wall had been bricked up, the work done so well that it was almost back to its original finish. "You can't even tell that someone ever broke through."

The team painted the high ceiling with their cellphone flashlight beams, searching for anything that even *suggested* a hiding place.

Tom checked out the centerpiece of the basement, the converted gas furnace, opening and closing its service doors and knocking around the exterior. *Nothing.* It just sat there, a giant, silent sentinel—stone cold to the touch. As Tom remembered, Charlie Varrick, the building's super, had told them that the furnace was rarely used in summer.

Meanwhile, the girls walked every foot of the dark floor stained by time, seeking any sign of a tunnel. Pete and Detective Ryan ran their hands over the sides of the four walls, hammering with clenched fists and listening for anything that sounded hollow. *Nothing.*

A good hour had passed when Detective Ryan's cellphone buzzed. After a brief discussion, he apologized and hurried off to another case. He handed the key to Suzanne. "Lock up when you leave."

The foursome gathered in a circle. "Now what?" Kathy asked.

Tom shrugged his shoulders in frustration. "Unless they

returned the day after the kidnapping, the money's just gotta be here . . . somewhere."

"They could easily have come back and helped themselves," Pete said. "I mean, why wouldn't they?"

"Hot money," Suzanne replied, "that's why." The Chief had taught his twins a thing or two.

Kathy tilted her head. "Hot money—what's that?"

"Holding onto three million bucks is a dangerous game," Tom explained. "Far better to leave it somewhere until things cool down. Some place safe . . . like down here." His eyes circled around.

"Oh, I get it," Pete said with a chuckle. "But you gotta admit, deserting stolen money at the scene of the crime has to be a first. One thing's for sure, they'll watch the dough like a hawk at dinnertime."

"You bet they will," Tom said. An idea had just taken shape in his mind. "And we'll be watching them."

14

PROVEN TECHNOLOGY

In a quick telephone call, Detective Joe Ryan approved their plan before disconnecting.

"I like it," he said. "Go for it."

"We gotta get in and out fast," Pete told the others. "Before Charlie Varrick or his assistant, Tim Smith, shows up."

Suzanne checked her phone. "That gives us a three-hour window to install the hardware."

Tom's idea was a tried-and-true one: deploy a hidden, high-definition video camera programmed to auto-capture still images *after* being triggered by a motion sensor. The sensor uses infrared radiation to detect light, which almost immediately changes temperature and causes the triggering event.

The camera also fired off alerts when it detected a change in its field of view, sending texts to all four of the mystery searchers cell phones, day or night. They had deployed the sophisticated device in the course of earlier adventures.

An hour later, they raced out to Ray Huntley's ranch to

pick up the hardware. Ray, president of the school's technology club, had often loaned high-tech tools from the club's arsenal to aid the foursome before.

"Who are you after this time?" he asked.

Kathy helped load the camera case into the Chevy's trunk. "You heard about the kidnapping?"

"Mrs. Walters? Did I ever. You involved with that one?

"We sure are," Pete said.

"Any leads?"

"We think so," Suzanne replied. "And this camera could make a real difference."

"Good for you," Ray said with a smile, waving goodbye. He knew not to ask too many questions about an ongoing case.

The mystery searchers biggest challenge centered around the hardware's installation. They settled on a location high on one wall, near the ceiling. A corner piece in the dusty rafter system, located diagonally across from the stairs, offered a wide-angle view of the entire space.

Kathy had estimated a floor-to-ceiling height at twelve feet.

"Wrong," Pete groused. He had inched his way up the stepladder they had rented earlier that day, stopping before the top two narrow steps. "It's at least fifteen feet up here . . . it sure looks like a long drop to the floor. This won't be easy." Pete was not at ease with heights—or enclosed spaces. But he knew that the only way to overcome his fears was to face them.

Tom and Suzanne served as ballast, weighing down each side of the ladder. Pete edged up one step higher before perilously stretching his arms up. Kathy crawled up just below him.

"Hammer," Pete said. His sister passed it up. *Bang, bang.*

He nailed a small aluminum harness onto the corner rafter. Difficult to do at that angle, but he did it.

"Camera." Pete slipped the device loaded with a charged high-capacity battery, into the harness, where it initially rested at a weird downward angle. He adjusted it carefully. The position held.

"Cardboard." Kathy thrust up a cone-shaped sleeve she had crafted that morning. Pete slipped it over the camera so that only the lens peeked out. The color of the cardboard matched the dirty brown color of the rafters. The overall construct faded into the shadowy ceiling; unless someone looked hard, they'd never see it.

"Okay, I got it." Pete took a deep breath. He took one step down.

"Turn it on first, Pete," Kathy said quietly.

"Well, duh." He stepped back up. Seconds later, *click.*

As they folded up the ladder, text alerts began arriving on all four cellphones. Pete grinned. "At least we know the darn thing works."

"Never a doubt," Tom said. "What time is it?"

"Four-fifteen," Suzanne replied.

"Perfect. Let's pack this ladder up and get out of here. Give me a hand, Pete."

"Sure. What are the chances the kidnappers show up tonight?"

"Fifty-fifty," Tom replied.

"Sixty-forty," Kathy said.

"I say seventy-thirty!" Suzanne said. "Depends how freaked out they are. If the story unsettles them, they'll show —quick."

. . .

89

THE DISTINCTIVE ALERT TONE—A QUIET *DING . . . DING . . . ding*—woke all four mystery searchers just after one o'clock in the morning.

"What time is it?" Tom muttered, jumping out of bed and grabbing his cell. He reached for his jeans.

"Who cares?" Suzanne replied in a soft voice from across the hall. *"This is great.* I'll message Joe Ryan, and Heidi too."

Meanwhile, Pete threw on his clothes and whispered to his sister, "Let's roll!"

Five minutes later, the foursome piled up outside the former bank's dark security door. Two other cars pulled up on the street and screeched to a halt. Special Agent Reilly and Detective Ryan hurried over, with Heidi right behind them. Suzanne inserted the key and swung open the door.

Tom flicked on the light switch and the seven descended, the officers leading, into the dimly lit basement with its single hanging bulb. Half-way down, distinctive alert tones rang out from the mystery searchers' four cellphones.

"Nice to know the camera's still doing its job," Kathy quipped.

The detective, Suzanne noticed, had pulled his handgun out of its holster.

"Nobody here," Reilly said with a trace of disappointment. "You're sure they came down?"

"Not 'they,'" Tom corrected him. *"He.* Check. It. Out."

Everyone peered over his shoulder as he touched the auto-alert app on his phone and hit play. Once triggered, the camera was programed to capture stills every ten seconds. The first still captured a surrealistic grey figure half-way down the stairs, wearing dark clothes and a baseball hat pulled low over his brow. It was impossible to see his face. He carried a flashlight projecting a weak beam downward. *He's illuminating the steps,* Tom thought.

"It's the mystery man!" Kathy exclaimed.

"Uh-huh, it surely is," Suzanne agreed.

"I bet he covered the lens with one hand," Pete murmured. "The light's peeking through his fingers."

A second frame popped up ten seconds later. The night-time visitor had already made his way into the basement and reached the far side of the furnace. A third image showed the mystery man at the foot of the stairs, about to head up. Then, nothing.

"Hang on," Special Agent Reilly exclaimed, his voice cracking a bit. He pushed closer to the screen. "He spent thirty seconds in the basement. *That's it?*"

"What the heck was he doing down here?" Detective Ryan asked, his eyes whipping around the cavernous space.

"Checking on the money," Suzanne said.

The idea seemed to stun everyone.

"Oh, sure," Pete blurted out. "You're right. I *get* it. The newspaper story turned up the heat and freaked him out. He was just making sure one of his partners hadn't blown town for parts unknown."

"With the money," Detective Ryan said, tugging at one ear. "Very plausible. Except that if the money is down here, where the heck is it?"

"No clue," Suzanne replied. "But now we know something else. There are two kidnappers in the city, maybe more. And they don't trust each other."

"That's a win for the good side," Heidi said.

Kathy giggled. "Whoever this guy is, he was afraid of an *unauthorized* withdrawal."

Everyone laughed. "Well, you could be right," Reilly said. "The cash has to be here somewhere. Eventually, one of them will come and try to grab it. Joe, can we set up overnight surveillance?"

"Sure. I'll arrange that for the next few nights. We'll hide an officer with a view of the street from midnight until morning."

"Yeah, that makes sense. This guy is a night crawler."

"And we'll leave our little camera in place," said Tom. "It could come in handy."

15

STAKEOUTS

Sunday morning, the Jackson and Brunelli families attended St. Francis Church. Later, they enjoyed lunch at their favorite eatery, a hole-in-the-wall Mexican restaurant, a shared family tradition dating back to when the four friends had been little kids.

"I mean, this is *authentic*," Pete said, smacking his lips.

While their parents caught up with one another, the four young detectives gathered at the other end of the table, quietly hatching plans over delicious plates of cheese enchiladas, bean tostadas, and chimichangas, covered in the blistering-hot salsa they all loved.

Beads of sweat popped out on Pete's forehead. "Man, I love this stuff," he said between bites.

A minute earlier, Tom had startled them with a question. "What happens if one of them takes a run at the cash in the evening hours?"

"No way," Kathy said. "Somebody would spot him."

"If it's the short guy," Suzanne argued, "he could care less.

He'd be wearing a disguise. I mean, nobody in Prescott even recognized him from his photo in the *Pilot*, right?"

"Right," Pete said, stuffing himself with chips and salsa.

"So what do we do now?" Kathy asked.

"How about setting up our own surveillance," Tom suggested. "I doubt if the gang would show in daylight hours, but evenings are a possibility. I'm thinking six p.m. until midnight."

"Where, how?" Pete asked.

Kathy hated stakeouts with a passion, but this one made sense. "That's easy. We'll call our buddy Lawrence and ask him if we can move into his pad . . . just for a few evenings. He's at work today and tomorrow."

"It's a big thing to ask," Suzanne agreed, "but I'm sure he won't mind."

"Okay," Tom said. He flipped a quarter in the air. "Call it, Pete."

"Heads."

"Heads it is. Your choice: tonight or Monday night?"

"Monday," Kathy said. "I hate stakeouts."

Pete yawned. "Whatever."

Sunday evening, nothing happened. Pure boredom . . . except that the Jacksons discovered that Lawrence liked to play earsplitting music nonstop. Apparently, the walls were thick and his neighbors were deaf—at least, he said, they never complained. Worse, Sunday was one of his days off.

"We forgot about that," Suzanne groused the next morning. "When midnight rolled around, I had one of the worst headaches of my life."

"I actually liked some of his music," Tom countered.

"You can have my share."

. . .

THE BRUNELLIS MOVED INTO LAWRENCE'S APARTMENT ON Monday, a few minutes ahead of six o'clock. Lawrence rushed away just as they arrived. "Technical problem at the hotel. See ya."

Kathy was ecstatic. "Lucky us—no music."

Pete pulled out a deck of cards. Gin rummy would lead off the evening while they took turns watching the street below.

When it came to stakeouts, time always dragged. It just did. Three hours passed before Pete yawned and glanced out the window. Again. For the umpteenth time. *Nothing.*

"Let's switch over to double solitaire," he challenged, pulling out a second deck. It was one of their favorite two-person card games. The object is to build eight "foundation" piles that each begin with an ace in ascending order to end with a king. A race to get rid of all your cards—the entire deck.

Soon enough, they were so involved—Pete was sure he'd win; in fact, he was always sure he'd win—that they hadn't spotted a car as it pulled into the loading zone. Then, distinctive alerts sounded on both phones: *ding . . . ding . . . ding.*

The siblings leapt to their feet. "There's a car in the loading zone!" Kathy shouted as she reached for her cell.

Pete couldn't believe it. Just then, the basement door pushed open from the inside. "Who the heck is it?"

Suzanne's cellphone buzzed. "Hi, Kathy. We heard the alerts. What's going on?"

"Hi, yourself. A little guy with a ponytail just dragged a box out of the basement and plunked it into a four-door Ford sedan." It was the first time the Brunellis had ever seen the man.

"Is he an older guy, looks like a weightlifter?"

"That's him."

"Charlie Varrick. No big deal—he works there."

"Except there's nothing down there—right?"

Suzanne put the call on speaker and glanced over to her brother. "Charlie Varrick is moving stuff out of the basement and into a car."

"Like what?"

"Like cardboard boxes," an animated Kathy said. "We were—I, uh—was winning at cards and we didn't spot him until the alerts went off."

"Are the boxes heavy?" Tom asked.

"The one we spotted sure was. Bet anything he's making a withdrawal."

Pete chuckled in the background. "Or closing down the account."

"He's going downstairs again," Kathy reported, her voice clipped.

Pete yelled something. "What did he say?" Suzanne asked.

"He said, 'Get over here, quick!'"

"We're on our way," Tom said. The twins had raced out the door and jumped into the Chevy.

On the way over, Suzanne began pulling up images from the camera. "Yup, it's Varrick all right. This one shows him hauling a box up the stairs. He's heading back down. . . now he's on the other side of the furnace. You know what this means, right?"

"Yup," Tom said. "It means Charlie Varrick might be the elusive mastermind. And he's one heck of an actor."

Three minutes passed in relative silence before Suzanne said, "We just drove past, Kathy. His Ford is still there, no sign of Mr. Varrick."

"Yeah, we spotted you. Just circle around and—*There he is!* He's got another heavy box. It's going into the back seat . . . no room in the trunk, maybe. Now he's returning to the service entrance and . . . nope, he's out . . . Betcha he locked up. He's in the driver's seat. I think . . . There he goes! *Where are you?*"

"Right behind him," Suzanne replied calmly.

"We need you to back us up!" Tom called out. "Otherwise, he'll realize someone's tailing him."

"We're on our way."

A game of follow-the-leader began. The Jacksons and Brunellis tag-teamed it, taking turns to tail Charlie Varrick along busy Highway 69, heading east toward Prescott Valley, a smaller city next door and the closest town to Prescott. All the while, conversation flowed back and forth on cellphone speakers in both cars.

"I don't get it," Kathy said. "Is Varrick the mystery man?"

"Not a chance," Suzanne said. "He's way too short. The mystery guy has some height to him, remember?"

Varrick managed to spend forty-five minutes on what would normally have been a twenty-minute drive.

"He's practicing evasive driving," Tom said, dropping back once more to let Pete take over. "It's a good thing the night works in our favor."

"I'll move up," Pete said. "He's heading into Prescott Valley. Someone Google him and see if you can find an address."

"I'm on it," Suzanne said.

Headlights illuminated both lanes of the highway, piercing the pitch-black night. Tom guided the white Chevy through heavy traffic. Every few minutes, the Mustang would shoot forward and take the lead, trying to stay within a few car lengths behind Charlie Varrick.

"He's being awfully careful," Kathy said at one point. "Look how he changes lanes back and forth."

"You bet he is," Suzanne replied. "I'm online searching for his— Here it is, *got him.* And here it is on Google Maps. Got his address. He should turn left at the next set of traffic lights. If he does, go straight, or he'll make us."

Sure enough, Varrick executed a hard left on a green arrow, right in the center of Prescott Valley. The mystery searchers' cars shot through the intersection before pulling neat three-point turns one after the other.

"Follow us," Suzanne told the Brunellis. Three blocks later, the two vehicles turned right into what appeared to be a small community laid out on both sides of a single long loop street. "He's number twenty-nine."

"I'm turning my lights off," Tom advised. In his rearview mirror, he watched the Mustang go dark too. The two sedans bumped along a rough gravel road.

Kathy counted down the address numbers. "Forty-three, forty-one, thirty-eight, thirty-five . . . *there*. . . twenty-nine, to the left. That's his place." Three homesteads farther along, an overhead light blazed up from the front of a tiny cottage-like home. A one-car garage appeared to the left of the house, its door closed.

"He must've parked in the garage," Suzanne said.

Tom pulled left into a vacant lot, a safe distance from number twenty-nine, leaving space for the Brunellis.

16

THE HOMESTEAD

In complete darkness, the mystery searchers crouched beside the Mustang and talked next moves.

"Time to call in the troops," Suzanne said, pulling out her cellphone.

"*Wait* a sec," Pete said. "How do we know he's home? He could've just circled the block while we were turning around back there. Maybe he's on his way to Alaska and left the light on to fake us out."

"*Alaska?*" His sister gave him some serious side-eye. "Where did that come from?"

"Just saying."

"Well, don't."

"Google says this is where he lives," Suzanne insisted. "The chances are pretty good he's in the garage counting money right now."

"What's your point, Pete?" Tom asked quietly.

"I don't like it. How stupid would we look if Varrick has already taken a hike?"

"Excuse me," Kathy protested. "We should have called Detective Ryan half an hour ago."

"What would he do?" Pete argued. "Just what we're doing —hanging around to see if another gang member shows. But he'd also creep over there and make sure Charlie Varrick's home. Which is precisely what I'm gonna do."

"Oh no you're not!" Kathy cried.

"You can't be serious!" Suzanne gasped. "Detective Ryan will skin us alive. We need to call him—*now.*"

"Watch me!" Pete bolted out from behind the car, crossed the gravel road, and jumped over an old wooden fence. He began the two-hundred-yard dash to the homestead, ducking low all the way.

Just as he reached the driveway, he triggered an automatic yard light.

"Oh, Lord," Kathy moaned.

An illuminated view of Varrick's cottage revealed a junkyard out front, with a couple of stripped-down cars wasting away in weeds. What appeared to be an old washing machine and a rust-stained dryer sat between them. It was easy to see that the bungalow had seen better days.

"Now *there's* a house that needs a paint job," Suzanne quipped.

Pete hustled over to the right side of the cottage. The other three held their collective breath—Kathy in mute terror—as her brother peered into a kitchen window. It appeared to have closed curtains, but he turned their way and gave a thumbs up: *Charlie's home.* He disappeared around the corner of the house. The yard light faded away. It took seconds for their eyes to adjust to the darkness, then . . . nothing.

The threesome waited for another three minutes before Suzanne touched the screen on her cellphone.

. . .

No sooner had Suzanne disconnected, when a dark-colored SUV came bumping along the rough road, headlights blazing. It drove past them, but they couldn't see anything in the darkened cabin. The vehicle turned into Varrick's driveway and stopped. The yard light glowed up as the SUV's lights cut away. A lone man slipped from the driver's seat on the vehicle's far side, his back to the trio as he hurried toward the house.

The front door swung open. *Varrick.* A shiver ran up and down Suzanne's spine. Something about the guy creeped her out. So, Varrick had been the mastermind all along! And here he was, front and center, caught in the soft glare of a yard light—the same individual who hesitantly walked down the basement stairs just days earlier. No stringy hair, no side-burns, sunken cheeks—a totally different face from the painter in Lawrence's video footage. He really was good at disguises.

The men shook hands before disappearing inside. The door closed, and the yard light faded away again.

By now, Kathy was in full panic mode. "We have to check on Pete. We just *have* to."

"Okay, let's roll," Tom said. "Make sure we don't trigger that darn motion detector. We'll come in from the kitchen side."

Suzanne rushed off with the others following close behind.

The trio traced Pete's footsteps, crossing the gravel roadway and slipping over a broken-down wooden fence. After hiking through a grassy area, they approached the cottage, inching their way up to the kitchen window and peeking between two curtains. The new arrival sat with his back to them. Varrick appeared angry or worried . . . or both. Raised voices carried through the glass.

No sign of Pete, Suzanne mouthed. She motioned to Tom and Kathy.

They circled to the rear to find a solid wooden door centered between large bedroom windows. Someone had blacked out the first window they came to; light streamed through broken-down curtains from the second one. A bed. A set of drawers. *But no Pete.*

They backed away, taking refuge behind a huge cottonwood.

"Varrick must have caught him," Suzanne whispered. "The troops won't be here for another ten minutes. What now?"

"A plan?" Kathy said hopefully.

"Ah, yes." Tom's mind plunged forward. "Kathy, you'll be the bait."

Her voice cracked. "Meaning *what,* exactly?"

"You run in front of Varrick's house, across the gravel road, and into that field. That'll trigger the motion detector on the yard light, making you visible. You stand out there, facing the creep. In fact, wave to him, taunt him—tick him off. Since you and Pete are lookalikes, especially at *that* distance, he only has two options."

"Oh, *I get it,*" Suzanne said quietly. "You'll confuse the heck out of him, Kathy. He'll either run to where Pete is, or chase you."

"Or both. And Kathy, you can outrun him, no problem. No way could he catch you."

She blinked in the dark. "I like your confidence."

"What about the mystery man?" Suzanne asked.

"Good question. All we can hope is that he follows

Varrick, otherwise . . ." He shrugged. "We have to do something."

"You're right," Kathy urged. "It's worth a try."

"Okay," Tom said. "Suzie, you and I'll hide out by the kitchen window and monitor them. Kathy, count to ten and take off. Make sure you cut into the driveway—that'll set off the yard light. Meet back at the car. Got it?"

"Got it."

Within seconds, Kathy ripped away at high speed, circling the house and racing down the driveway. The yard light flipped on as she crossed the gravel road, jumped another wooden fence, and headed deep into a grassy field. Then she turned, ready and wary.

The twins watched with bated breath as the men leapt up from the kitchen table and bolted to the front door. One of them yelled, "Hey, what the—! He got free! Get him!"

It's working! thought the twins.

The two men hightailed it out to the spot from which Kathy was now long gone. Tom and Suzanne raced through the open front door and down a hallway.

"Here," Suzanne cried out softly. Pete lay on the floor in the darkened back bedroom, his grateful eyes wide open, trussed up like a turkey, hands and feet tied and his mouth taped shut. A large gob of blood decorated the crown of his head. Suzanne yanked off the strip of duct tape with a single pull, which caused Pete to squelch a painful cry.

"That hurt," he whispered hoarsely. "What took you so long?"

"Nice to see you too," Suzanne retorted.

Tom untied his hands and feet, and the twins pulled him to a standing position. *"Move fast,"* Suzanne said, pushing him toward the back door. The three bolted out, past the cotton-woods, over another fence . . . to freedom.

REVELATIONS

The trio pivoted back to the vacant lot to find Kathy hunkered down on the far side of the Mustang, still catching her breath.

"Where have you been?" she joked, giving her brother a hug. "You okay?"

"I'm fine. My head hurts. He whacked me a good one."

"Didn't you see him coming?"

"*Are you kidding?* Of course I didn't. Where were you hiding?"

"Hiding? *Are you serious?* I was an integral part of the rescue team."

"That's a fact," Suzanne said. "Good job, Kathy. Did they even get close to you?"

"Nope. I waved bye-bye and never looked back."

The twins explained how the extraction had unfolded.

"Thanks," Pete said. He meant it too. "Did you guys spot the ransom money?"

"We sure didn't," Suzanne said. "I'll bet anything it's still in Varrick's car."

Tom craned his neck over to the homestead. "Hey, the yard light's back on. There's activity on the driveway. Where the heck is Detective Ryan?"

Suzanne glanced at her cellphone. "Any minute now. Did anyone notice the duck?"

"The duck?" Pete asked.

"Yup. The mystery man—the guy with the duck walk. I spotted it when he hustled out with Varrick."

"Seriously?" Pete asked, incredulous.

"Serious."

"They're leaving!" Tom yelled. Two cars backed out of the driveway and sped off in the opposite direction, away from the foursome. The sound of multiple sirens pierced the air.

Suzanne grabbed her cellphone and touched a number on the screen. Heidi answered on the first ring.

THE MYSTERY SEARCHERS PULLED UP BEHIND THE KIDNAPPERS' cars, smack into a nighttime scene of organized chaos. Half a dozen police vehicles, all parked at odd angles, had boxed in the entrance to the gravel-paved loop street. A luminous crescendo of throbbing blue lights flickered eerily into the night, bouncing off houses and trees. Sound from multiple two-way radios crackled nonstop.

The police had stopped the kidnappers from accessing the main road. Varrick's sedan sat nose-to-nose with a ghost car, its doors and trunk splayed wide open. Uniformed police and plain-clothed detectives milled around, staring at four enormous boxes of money. A murmur of voices cut softly into the night.

So did Pete. *"That's* what millions of bucks looks like."

Officers had already escorted Charlie Varrick and the

mystery man, both handcuffed, into the back seats of separate cruisers.

The mystery searchers caught up with Detective Ryan and FBI Special Agent Reilly just as the Chief arrived on the scene and strode over. The first words out of his mouth were, "Are you okay, Pete?"

"Oh, yeah. I'm fine, Chief, thank you." He touched the crown of his head gingerly. "No problem at all. Just a slight knock here."

The Chief grunted. "Glad to hear it. Your parents are on their way."

The Brunellis shot each other their brother-sister *Oh-oh* look. Pete, they knew, had just landed in big trouble.

"We got 'em both?" the Chief asked.

"Sure did," Agent Reilly replied, pointing toward two patrol cars. "Right there."

"Who's the mystery man?"

"It's a surprise," Detective Ryan said, indicating the closest vehicle. As usual, his expression revealed nothing.

"I don't like surprises," the Chief growled. He strode over to the car, opened the rear passenger door, and bent over. "Why, Ben! What brings you out to this neck of the woods?"

Ben Walters turned away, refusing eye contact. "I need to see my attorney."

"You certainly do," the Chief replied dryly. "And I'll make sure that happens." He closed the door and turned back to everyone. "Corporate malfeasance. Fraud. Embezzlement. Lying to the Bureau. Lots of charges."

"Of course. It makes so much sense!" Pete said. "I mean, the guy kidnapped his own wife—who would ever suspect him?"

"Yes," Suzanne said. "That explains something that has bugged me all along."

"Like what?" Tom asked.

"Like the kidnappers having food waiting for her in the motel, including her favorite treat: glazed chocolate doughnuts. I mean, what are the odds? They *knew* about her. They didn't want to frighten her, and they took care of her—because they had been told they had to."

Pete smiled wryly. "Huh. Mr. Walters was looking after her all along, right?"

"Darren Baker is on his way," Reilly informed the Chief. "He should arrive in about an hour."

"Got it, thanks."

Another car pulled up with a screech of brakes. Heidi Hoover jumped out and sprinted over, her curls bouncing, pulling out her oversize notebook on the fly.

ANOTHER DEBRIEFING—WITH A VICTORY LAP

Two days later, Detective Ryan and Special Agent Reilly invited "all interested parties" to the station for a debriefing session: *10:00 a.m. sharp at police headquarters,* read the text. The blockbuster case—Prescott's only kidnapping for ransom that anyone could remember—drew a crowd, forcing a move to a large training room.

The Chief and Darren Baker sat in the front row with Ryan and Reilly, while Heidi and the mystery searchers gathered behind them. A special guest had tagged along with them: Lawrence Perrault, dressing sharply in a clean long-sleeved shirt and jeans.

And shoes and socks, Suzanne thought. *Could be a first.*

The Brunelli parents walked in together with Sherri and grabbed seats behind a handful of interested citizens.

Uniformed officers lined both sides of the room. Because the dramatic story had drawn national attention, a dozen out-of-town media types had congregated toward the back. Three television cameras focused on the front of the training room.

The Chief rose and stepped over to a podium before clearing his voice. "Okay, we're ready, folks. Thanks for coming. Our goal today is to brief everyone on the successful hunt for the elusive mastermind, the man behind the Walters kidnapping. I'd like to start by introducing the officers and agents who worked on the case. Then I have an opening statement before we accept questions."

Five minutes later, Heidi—*Who else?* thought Kathy— asked the first question. "Based on your comments, Chief, I assume Ben Walters is cooperating, is that correct?"

"Yes. He has held nothing back at all. But Varrick has lawyered up and refuses to talk with us."

"What possessed Walters to rob his own bank?"

"And kidnap his own wife," Kathy hastened to add.

The Chief yielded the podium to the two FBI agents. "Over the last year," Darren Baker answered, "Mr. Walters embezzled and lost $750 thousand dollars of the bank's money gambling online. He had reached a point when he could no longer hide his losses. That's when he recruited Charlie Varrick. He had met the man when Westward Bank had taken ownership of the historic bank building in a repo after the previous owner declared bankruptcy. Then, three years later, the bank sold it off to a developer in Los Angeles."

"Back then," Agent Reilly added, "Varrick bragged to Walters about his past, about how he was a master of disguises and had connections with the New York under- world from his years in the circus. Mr. Walters didn't give it a lot of thought—until he needed help."

"Who came up with the complicated plot to steal the money?" Maria Brunelli asked.

"Charlie Varrick. He's the elusive mastermind. Walters's idea was to pull off a nighttime robbery. Instead, Varrick proposed the kidnapping-and-ransom scheme and developed the elaborate plan. Walters was desperate—he knew he was in deep trouble, so he decided to go for it."

"Which proves an old adage," Darren Baker noted. "The best way to rob a bank is to own a bank. Or in this case, to run one."

Lawrence Perreault surprised the mystery searchers by raising his hand. "Charlie Varrick . . . is that his actual name? And how did he become a master of disguises?"

Detective Ryan rose to the podium. "Yes, to your first question. But Mr. Varrick hid his work history from us. He claimed he had been a handyman for a traveling circus. That checked out. But he neglected to tell us he also served as an acrobat and a clown for all the shows. He knew all about disguises."

"Can you confirm that Mrs. Walters had nothing to do with the crime?" Sherri asked.

"Yes, I can," Baker replied. "And I hasten to mention that her husband went to great lengths to protect Mrs. Walters. She is innocent and just as shocked as the rest of us. But she's standing by her man and doing her level best to help him out. I expect a judge will set bail and release him to his wife soon."

Joe Brunelli spoke up next, sounding astonished. "You mean he won't get locked up?"

"Not before the trial, no sir. After that, no telling. Walters has no criminal record and has enjoyed a stellar reputation in the bank and in the Prescott community."

"Boy, you can only imagine their kitchen table talk," Kathy whispered.

Someone else in the crowd who neither the Brunellis nor the Jacksons knew said, "I understand the kidnappers hid the money in the basement of the old bank building. *Where exactly did they hide it?*"

"In the hot air conduits," Detective Ryan replied. "And we should have figured that out. The kidnappers had set the furnace's main switch to the off position. When the weather cooled down a few days ago and the tenants couldn't get any heat, they started complaining to the super—Varrick. He lied to them, claiming he needed parts that were a week out."

Tom groaned. He recalled the stone-cold furnace, but the reason why it was so cold had never dawned on him. He had missed the turned-off switch. "Anything more on the two kidnappers who snatched Mrs. Walters?" he asked.

The FBI agents glanced at each other before Reilly replied. "A New York informant told our field office about a rumor circulating in the city. The story is that a couple of unnamed mafia members had pulled off a big heist in Arizona. We're still working the case, but it's unlikely we'll ever identify them."

Heidi raised a hand again. "You recovered some of the ransom money, correct?"

"Correct," Reilly replied. "One-point-five million dollars, exactly."

"No chance of recovering the other half?"

"Slim. The two plotters disguised as painters hauled it off in a cargo van on the afternoon of the kidnapping. We know the names they went by during the kidnapping, because Mrs. Walters told us: Tony and Russell. She said they both had Bronx accents. They took half the money and left town—presumably heading home to rejoin the mafia in New York."

The mystery searchers exchanged glances with Lawrence. So there *had* been money in the paint cans, after all. *A lot* of money.

Joe Brunelli almost went apoplectic. "You mean—you

can't be serious. Their fee was one and a half million dollars? *And they got away with it?"*

"I'm afraid so, sir," Darren Baker answered. "This time. Eventually, their luck will run out. It's only a matter of time."

Tom whistled quietly to himself. *Wow.*

"Who built the tunnel from the basement to the dumpster?" Heidi asked.

"Charlie Varrick, with help from the Bronx boys. Took them several days of slow, hard, patient work, using only hand tools, with Varrick supervising and doing the heavy lifting. Nothing to it, with his background. And he's as strong as an ox."

"No kidding," Pete muttered. "The guy carried me into the house like a sack of potatoes."

"Wouldn't people wonder about all the activity, and ask about the noise?" Sherri asked.

"Sure," Reilly replied. "But Varrick would just sluff it off. He could say he was 'fixing stuff' in the basement if anyone asked, but apparently almost no-one did. That's his job, after all—fixing stuff. In the daytime hours, the residential tenants are mostly off at work. And the retail tenants never come near the service entrance. Apparently, the hardest part was breaking through the pavement in the service alley. They did that late at night, as quiet and careful as possible."

"What did Varrick do with all the debris from the excavation?" Sherri asked.

"It was simple," said the Chief. "Walters told us the gang just put all the dirt and broken bricks in extra-heavy-duty industrial trash bags, a small amount at a time, and dropped right in the dumpster every night. The trash haulers took it all away, never the wiser."

"Wow," Sherri said. "Talk about convenient!"

"That's a fact," added Reilly. "And Varrick waited to cut

the holes up through the pavement and the bottom of the dumpster until the last minute, the night before the kidnapping, so the hauling company workers wouldn't see the tunnel. They had to cut the metal by hand to keep the work quiet, using an old-fashioned hand drill and a hacksaw with a tough bi-metal blade. And the debris from that last night's work—the broken bits of pavement and the jagged piece of metal from the floor of the dumpster—that they hauled off in the cargo van so the dumpster would be empty the next day for the ransom drop-off. Very clever."

"Okay," Detective Ryan asked, "Any more questions?"

"Just one," Maria Brunelli said. "What will happen to Charlie Varrick?"

Reilly coughed once before answering. "If he's found guilty, which in my opinion is likely, he'll probably spend the rest of his life behind bars."

A collective hush fell over the room.

Ryan and Reilly found their seats as the Chief rejoined Darren Baker at the podium.

"Okay," the Chief said. "We have several people that the FBI and Prescott City Police want to thank, including the two investigators in charge, Special Agent Jim Reilly and Detective Joe Ryan. Please stand once more, gentlemen." A round of applause burst out.

"Thank you. Outstanding work, indeed. You had a lot of help from Heidi Hoover and *The Daily Pilot*. Where are you, Heidi?"

The diminutive reporter waved from her seat. The thing she hated most was the limelight—she took the old-fashioned view that the reporter should never become the story —but people clapped anyway.

"We're very appreciative, Heidi. You made all the difference. Please let your management know how grateful we are. Is there a young man here named Lawrence Perrault?"

The self-described geek stood and waved.

"I'm told that without your help we wouldn't have caught Charlie Varrick," Darren Baker said. "Your surveillance camera footage proved invaluable—we owe you a debt of gratitude." More clapping.

"And last, we have Prescott's own mystery searchers, the foursome who tracked the kidnappers right to Varrick's home in Prescott Valley. A special thanks to Pete Brunelli, a team member who strayed out on a limb to discover that Varrick was indeed home on the night of his arrest. Please stand, the four of you."

Applause and cheers broke out. Pete glanced over at his parents, pleased to see they had joined in with the crowd. A half-smile crossed his sister's face. *Whew.*

Later, after the meeting ended, people milled around, talking in small groups. At one point, Travis and Tina Johnson stepped over to the mystery searchers and introduced themselves. Travis explained he had been working at Westward Bank for a year. "Pretty weird. I go on vacation and one of the biggest heists in Prescott history hits the bank."

"We figured you as a suspect," Pete admitted.

Travis laughed. "So did the FBI. We had to fly home to clear ourselves."

"Thank God for passport stamps," Tina said.

It was close to noon. The Brunellis and their parents conversed with Ryan and Reilly. Meanwhile, Darren Baker had cornered the Chief, Sherri, and their twins.

"Great job," he said, addressing Tom and Suzanne. "I liked the way you refused to give up. That made all the difference. What's next for the mystery searchers?"

Suzanne smiled and caught her best friend's eye. "Nothing huge. Tomorrow Kathy and I are going shopping."

"Tennis," Tom said with a grin. He swung one arm, simulating his best serve. "Pete and I . . . first thing in the morning."

The Chief coughed once. "Uh-huh. After the fence, of course."

"The fence?"

"Yup. Remember? It's in awful shape and needs your skills."

The twins gawked at one another in dismay.

Suzanne mouthed, "We're cooked."

Did you enjoy the book? Please leave a review!
And check out a snippet of book 9 on the next page.

EXCERPT FROM BOOK 9

THE LEGEND OF RATTLER MINE

Vultures!

The mystery searchers raced their horses to the northern border of the Flying W Dude Ranch. They pulled up, side by side, their mounts panting, on a bluff overlooking undulating meadowlands broken by a series of canyons and ravines. The picture-perfect scenes before them were stunning.

"Wow," Suzanne exclaimed. "Check. It. Out."

Meadow grass rustled in the breeze like silken waves. In the distance, mountains reached high into a brilliant sky as huge, puffy white clouds sailed across an ocean of Arizona blue. To the west, ponderosa pines arose, countless green sentinels that filled their eyes as far as they could see. At the bottom of the sharp drop-off below the bluff, cottonwoods dotted both sides of a running creek, too distant for them to hear the bubbling water.

They breathed deeply, enjoying the cool, fresh air that wafted down from the northern heights, carried by a gusting wind. No one said a word as they passed two canteens back and forth. Overhead, birds wheeled and screeched in the early afternoon. Their horses whinnied and stamped their hooves, eager to move on.

That's when Pete Brunelli startled everyone, pointing into the sky, and shouting, "Vultures!" Half a mile away, three raptors soared in wobbly circles above the rolling meadows, their wings tilted high enough to resemble a letter V.

"*E-e-e-ew*," Kathy exclaimed, pulling a face. "You're right. Nature's garbagemen! They're circling in for a landing. Has to be roadkill down there . . . somewhere. Yuck."

Born and raised in Central Arizona, the foursome knew all about the unsightly birds. Although their vast wingspan allowed them to fly and glide with a mere twitch of a wing, they weren't quite as graceful in defending themselves. The raptors' only defense against predators was to vomit all over them. And considering that they only eat dead meat, well . . .

"*Roadkill?* No way," Pete replied, never reluctant to argue with his sister. "There isn't a road for miles. Who's got the binoculars?"

The twins, Tom and Suzanne Jackson, glanced at each other. "I do," Suzanne said. She reached into her saddlebags and retrieved a set. Within seconds, she focused on the three vultures as they continued to hover, riding thermals in wide circles. Two species of the birds make Arizona their summer home, and they're quite similar.

"What are they, Suzie?" Tom asked. He was the thoughtful, quiet one of the four.

"Turkey vultures." Through the binoculars, the species was easily identifiable by its bald, red head and pinkish bill, and a black-and-grey wingspan that could often exceed five feet. Suzanne knew that they migrated north from Mexico every spring and returned in the fall—and that they can smell carrion from an incredible eight miles away. She handed the binoculars to Pete.

Kathy held one hand out toward her brother. "Gimme." He ignored her for the longest time, earning a withering look.

Then, without warning, Pete—always the impulsive one —nudged the flanks of his fast, chestnut-colored gelding and galloped off, shouting, "Let's go see what they're after!"

The mystery searchers had won a week's stay at the Flying W, located a few miles northwest of Prescott. Heidi Hoover—a good friend and the star reporter of *The Daily Pilot*, Prescott's hometown newspaper—had recommended the foursome for the prize. Their work on solving a recent kidnapping-and-ransom case had made national headlines. With a little help from Heidi, the four had helped track down the crime's elusive mastermind.

The *Pilot* had awarded its Citizen of the Year Award to the four friends. It was the first time the paper had ever honored a group rather than an individual with the much-coveted prize. The mystery searchers couldn't believe their luck.

"I *love* horses," Suzanne had said when Heidi called to share the good news. "I can't wait!"

A grin crossed Tom's face. "The ranch's wranglers are known for working their guests half to death."

"I can handle it." She could too. Often when friends thought of the outgoing girl, one word came to mind: *confident*. She knew where she was going in life, and how to get there.

Prescott, a small Central Arizona city nestled in a mile-high basin among pine-dotted mountains, boasts hundreds of miles of riding trails. It's also home to "the world's oldest rodeo"—cowboy country, for sure.

As the foursome had soon discovered, a week at the Flying W Dude Ranch was no picnic. Rather, it was an intensive course on how to feed, water, groom, saddle and bridle, mount, ride, walk, trot, canter, and dismount a horse. *Whew!*

Now Friday had arrived, along with their final ride. Each of them had admitted to loving every minute of the experience. Or most of it, anyway. Cleaning up after the horses in the barn—mucking out their stalls—wasn't as much fun as riding them and handing out treats.

"It hasn't all been peaches and cream," Kathy reminded her brother—her favorite target for good-natured teasing—with a giggle. "Remember when you fell off Trigger?"

Pete chortled. "Time out! Trigger and I are old friends now."

In a way, that was true. The Flying W wranglers had paired each of them with their own mount for the duration. Horse and rider had soon grown to know each other, and what to expect. Best of all, the dude ranch reserved mornings for chores and riding lessons. Afternoons were free for riding the range from one o'clock on. *Delicious.*

Pete led, yipping and yahooing down the left side of the bluff and onto the meadowlands. Trigger coursed across familiar territory as he galloped over the grasslands without a second's hesitation, heading toward endless canyons and ravines that gathered in front. As they grew closer to the first ravine, the horse slowed.

"Hold up, Pete!" his sister yelled from behind. Kathy's dark-bay quarter horse was a gentle beast that liked to ramble rather than run. All Kathy had to say was "Whoa," and he slowed to a halt.

The twins, riding a pair of young mares—Tom's a palomino he had nicknamed Goldie, and his sister's a strawberry roan—caught up with their best friends. "Check out the birds," Suzanne said. "They're still circling. What are they waiting for?"

"Dinner," Kathy quipped. "And whatever's on the menu isn't far away."

Tom cut to the right, heading northeast, searching for a safe path around a steep, narrow gorge that appeared risky. The foursome traveled together in silence as the sure-footed horses trotted along. A few hundred yards farther on, the gorge merged into a navigable, rock-filled chasm with gently sloping sides that soon returned them to the meadowlands.

"Hooray!" Pete yelled, leaving the others in a cloud of dust.

Minutes later, the horses began slowing once more as another ravine lay ahead. The raptors were almost directly overhead now, still circling, gradually working their way lower. The four riders dismounted and walked closer to the edge.

Kathy stopped dead in her tracks as she peered down into the abyss. One hand flew to her mouth. "Oh, my Lord. There's a body down there—a human body!"

Suzanne blanched. "There surely is."

Pete and Tom gazed down, jolted into silence.

The steep ravine wall slanted downward at a sharp angle. Right at the bottom, maybe fifteen yards down, lay a heavy-set, bareheaded man with a bushy red beard, face up, one arm folded over his chest, the other resting at his side. He wore jeans and a long-sleeved shirt.

"Looks like he's sleeping," Kathy said.

Pete shook his head. "Naw, I think he's a goner."

"I doubt it," Tom said. He grabbed a rope attached to his saddle and looped the strap of a canteen around his neck.

"Why not?" Pete asked.

"The vultures, remember? They only eat carrion. And they haven't landed. Yet."

"Oh, got it," Pete replied. "I'm going down with you."

"No way," Suzanne said. "You're riding the fastest horse. No matter whether the guy's dead or alive, we'll need help. Tom and I'll handle it."

"What the heck," Pete objected. "That's what cellphones are for. It's called nine-one-one."

"Good luck with that, buddy," Kathy retorted, whipping her phone out of her pocket to check for a signal. "Cellphone service out here in the meadowlands is pretty patchy, and right here . . . zip."

"Well, that's awkward," Pete said, disappointment heavy in his voice. That hadn't crossed his mind. *"Duh."*

Tom tied one end of the rope to a dead tree on the edge of the ravine. "It'll get us down ten feet at the most, but it's a good start."

Broken rocks of every shape and size lined the ravine's walls, protruding from the packed earth. The twins used them for footholds as they climbed down, testing each one before putting weight on it. A few smaller rocks pushed loose and thundered downhill, one almost rolling over the helpless man.

"Geez," Tom muttered to himself. "That was close."

Three minutes later, they fell to their knees before the red-bearded man. He appeared to be in his fifties, unconscious, and badly hurt.

But alive.

"He's still breathing," Suzanne murmured, watching his chest rise and fall. "But pale as a ghost." His forehead felt cool to the touch.

The twins noticed bloody abrasions on the man's head, neck, arms, and hands. A great deal of blood had pooled below his upper back. Worse, it had begun coagulating along one side.

"He must have rolled down into the ravine," Tom said. "And recently too."

Suzanne agreed. "Fallen . . . or been pushed. His clothes are damp. How come?"

"Might be sweat from being out in the sun. How on earth would he get all the way out here? We're so far from —anywhere."

"Maybe he came on horseback, like us, but his horse ran off," Suzanne said.

Tom unscrewed the canteen lid and poured a tiny amount of water over the man's lips. He shuddered as his eyes flickered open. A few seconds passed before he focused on Suzanne's face. He struggled to speak, licking his lips. The twins leaned closer.

"I—I, uh . . . It's there . . . I found it . . ." His eyes flickered once more, then closed.

For one horrifying moment, Suzanne thought he had died. But he continued to breathe in shallow gasps.

Tom lifted the man's arms one at a time, gently palpating his chest and the sides of his ribcage with the fingertips of one hand. *Nothing.* He slid his hands under both shoulders and felt around.

Suzanne swiveled her head and glanced up at the Brunellis, peering down from the top of the ridge. She cupped her mouth, shouting, *"He's alive!* And hurt badly! We need a medical helicopter—but it won't be able to land in the ravine!"

"Tell 'em they'll have to lower a stretcher down there," Kathy said to her brother.

"Okay, I'm on it!" Pete yelled back. He bounded into his saddle.

"And while you're at it, call Sheriff McClennan!" Tom called out. *"Somebody shot this guy!"* I hope you have enjoyed this sneak peek at book 9 in the

Mystery Searchers Book series

The Legend of Rattlesnake Mine

To be released in fall 2021

BIOGRAPHY

Barry Forbes began his writing career in 1980, eventually scripting and producing hundreds of film and video corporate presentations, winning a handful of industry awards along the way. At the same time, he served as an editorial writer for Tribune Newspapers and wrote his first two books, both non-fiction.

In 1997, he founded and served as CEO for Sales Simplicity Software, a market leader which was sold two decades later.

What next? "I always loved mystery stories and one of my favorite places to visit was Prescott, Arizona. It's situated in rugged central Arizona with tremendous locales for mysteries." In 2017, Barry merged his interest in mystery and his skills in writing, adding in a large dollop of technology. The Mystery Searchers Family Book Series was born.

Barry's wife, Linda, passed in 2019 and the series is dedicated to her. "Linda proofed the initial drafts of each book and acted as my chief advisor." The couple had been married for 49 years and had two children. A number of their fifteen grandchildren provided feedback on each book.

Contact Barry: barry@mysterysearchers.com

BOOK 3: THE SECRETS OF THE MYSTERIOUS MANSION

Heidi Hoover, a good friend and the star newspaper reporter for the *Daily Pilot*, Prescott's local newspaper, introduces the mystery searchers to a mysterious mansion in the forest—at midnight! The mansion is under siege from unknown "hunters." Who are they? What are they searching for? Good old-fashioned detective work and a couple of hi-tech tools ultimately point toward the truth, but time is running out . . .

BOOK 4: THE HOUSE ON CEMETERY HILL

There's a dead man walking, and it's up to the mystery searchers to figure out why. That's the challenge laid down by Mrs. Leslie McPherson, a successful but eccentric Prescott businesswoman. The mystery searchers team up with their favorite local detective and use some hi-tech gadgets to spy on some equally high-tech criminals at Cemetery Hill. It's a perilous game—with very high stakes.

BOOK 5: THE TREASURE OF SKULL VALLEY

Suzanne discovers a map hidden in the pages of an old classic book at the thrift store where she works. It's titled "My Treasure Map" and leads past Skull Valley, twenty miles west of Prescott, and out into the high desert country—to an unexpected treasure. "Please help," a note on the map begs. The mystery searchers rely on the power and reach of the internet to trace the movement of people and events—from half a century earlier.

BOOK 6: THE VANISHING IN DECEPTION GAP

A text message to Kathy sets off a race into the unknown. "There are pirates operating out here, and they're dangerous. I can't prove it but I need your help." Who sent the message? Out where? Pirates! In a railway yard? The mystery searchers dive in, but it might be too late. The sender has vanished into thin air.

BOOK 7: THE GETAWAY LOST IN TIME

A stray dog saves the twins from a dangerous predator on the hiking trail at Watson Lake. In a surprising twist, the dog leads the mystery searchers to the suspicious recent death of Hilda Wyndham—and a crime lost to the passage of time. They join the Sheriff's Office of Yavapai County and Heidi Hoover, the star reporter of the *Daily Pilot*, in a search for unknown perpetrators past and present.

BOOK 8: THE HUNT FOR THE ELUSIVE MASTERMIND

The mystery searchers embark on one of their strangest cases—the kidnapping of the wife of one of Prescott's most prominent bankers. The mystery deepens as baffling questions emerge: Who are the kidnappers—beneath their disguises? What happened to the ransom money? And it soon becomes clear that the hostage may not be the only person in danger . . .

BOOK 9: THE LEGEND OF RATTLER MINE – COMING FALL, 2021

On the last day of a glorious week at the Flying W Dude Ranch, the mystery searchers and their horses enjoy a final, exhilarating ride across Central Arizona's meadowlands. Soon, they spot a trio of circling vultures, floating on thermals and slowly descending into the next ravine. Suzanne wonders, "What do you think they're waiting for?" Kathy quipped, "Dinner. And whatever's on the menu isn't far away." Pete yells, "Let's go!" What awaited the mystery searchers was something—and somebody—most unexpected.

BOOK 10: THE HAUNTING OF THE HASSAYAMPA –
COMING SPRING, 2022

In progress!

READER STUDY GUIDES

Don't forget to check out
www.MysterySearchers.com

to receive *free* parent/teacher-and-reader study guides for each book in the series—valuable teaching and learning tools for middle-grade students and their parents or teachers.

You'll also find a wealth of information on the website, including stills and video scenes of Prescott, reviews, press releases, rewards, and more. Plus updates on new releases and other Mystery Searchers news.

You can also connect with me via the Mystery Searchers website. I *love* to hear from my readers—of any age.

—Barry Forbes